I've absolutely laughed myself silly reading this. I can identify so much with it that it could be about me. I had caesareans and felt exactly the same and my first outing to an NCT coffee morning was pretty much the same as Sarah's. It's a very easy read, the sort you could enjoy round the pool on holiday - which is a good thing. I love Sarah's conversational tone. She's a very likeable character and I found myself wanting to stick with her to see how things worked out.

Melanie La Vie, Authonomy

Well well well. What have got here? A tsunami of excitement. I particularly laughed when you talked about sex and said no one would read it, knowing we all reading it. You are funny. Good stuff, you should write part two!

Jenny Hill, Authonomy

This is an enjoyable and effortless read that subtly uses humour to look at the ever increasing complexities of being a single mum. The insight into Sarah's imagination as she dealt with 'the other woman', the stigma of being a 'poor' lone parent and the determination to transform her life all resonate; funny yet so true!

Claire Gillman, editor and author of *The Best of Boys* (Pan)

Any woman who has ever felt betrayal will surely resonate with this book. Sarah's life is turned upside down by the man she loves. She is initially lost in a sea of emotions. This read touches your heart and soul and serves as a reminder that life seldom stays the same but with humour it shows us life can and does go on.

Annette Greenwood, Life Coach and author of *Imprisoned Heart*

Being
Sarah Chilton

(A guide for all Mums when
the sh*t hits the fan)

Being
Sarah Chilton

(A guide for all Mums when
the sh*t hits the fan)

R. E. Briddon

**SASSY
BOOKS**

Winchester, UK
Washington, USA

First published by Sassy Books, 2013
Sassy Books is an imprint of John Hunt Publishing Ltd., Laurel House, Station Approach,
Alresford, Hants, SO24 9JH, UK
office1@jhpbooks.net
www.johnhuntpublishing.com
www.sassy-books.com

For distributor details and how to order please visit the 'Ordering' section on our website.

Text copyright: R. E. Briddon 2011

ISBN: 978 1 78099 818 3

A CIP catalogue record for this book is available from the British Library.

Design: Stuart Davies

This book is entirely a work of fiction. The name of the characters and incidents portrayed in it
are the work of the author's imagination. Any resemblance to actual persons, living or dead,
events and localities, are entirely coincidental.

Printed and bound by CPI Group (UK) Ltd, Croydon, CR0 4YY

We operate a distinctive and ethical publishing philosophy in all
areas of our business, from our global network of authors to
production and worldwide distribution.

CONTENTS

To Elizabeth and Elaine Banner
Forever in my thoughts xx

Foreword

Life is like a game of cards. The hand that is dealt you represents determinism; the way you play it is free will.
Jawaharal Nehru

For years I've had this nagging feeling to collate my diaries and publish them. Nothing new in that you may think, I am not the only one to have been through the wringer in this life, nor will I be the last, so in many ways I am just a statistic... But the reason I wanted to put it out in a book was to let others know that you are not alone when life doesn't pan out the way you had hoped. I am brutally honest about my thoughts and feelings. And as my diaries spanned many years, I have kept only the most poignant, funny, sad, and downright outrageous bits. My hope is that you finish this book feeling enlightened, inspired and having had a bloody good laugh with me and at me!

Love Sarah

Introduction

My parents moved down to Brixham in the 1960s to escape the smoke of the Midlands. They bought a split-level bungalow with a breathtaking view of farmers' fields in the higher part of the town. They were so desperate to move to Brixham and fell in love with the view but my Mum said 'Who buys a house with the bedrooms downstairs? Bloody stupid idea, I'll stick it two years Jim'. Countless years later she's still there. It's my home and I love it. My Dad had an affair and left Mum, my elder Sister, Jayne, and I on our own. I say '*an* affair', he had many over the years, but this affair was the one that broke the camel's back and Mum threw him out. 'You can't leave, you're my Daddy and I love you too much' is a very vivid memory for me, just eight, and one that has stayed for a long time. She was called Denise. Having seen how it affected Mum, I promised myself to not let this happen to me. I've not had much luck with men thus far. I'm not the best looking grape on the vine. I'm the one that gets left on it and chucked away. I was never in the 'it gang' at school and my confidence wasn't exactly boosted when boys would refer to me as 'ginger nut' or 'Duracell' due to the prominent, and ridiculously thick, red hair I inherited from my Great Great Grandfather. All I wanted was to blend in at school, but oh no, I was the one with the red hair and really bad 'Mum's DIY' haircut. One of the worst knock backs was when the boys laughed at my dancing at the lunchtime disco when I was fourteen. I think I just gave up and realised that this grape would never ripen and would end up a shrivelled up sultana.

Anyway, back to Brixham. It's a bit like living in a large cul-de-sac. Once you arrive in the town it's a dead end. You don't pass through on your way to somewhere else. You go for a reason. It comprises of your normal tourist attractions; fish and chip shops, amusement arcades, shops full of holiday 'tat' and pubs. It's a thriving fishing port and is known throughout Europe. I'm very proud of my home town. There are a few remaining businesses who have survived the recession and I work for one of them. I'm a secretary for an accountant and it's a bit dull to be honest. There are six of us in the office, none of whom I've got anything in common with. It's an old terraced house, spread over four floors, on the main road, which was converted into offices by the current owner, Mr Mosson, complete and utter wanker, literally, so I call him 'Toss on'. He has a drawer in his office full to the brim with porn magazines. He's a rotund man who would roll if he fell over. He thinks it perfectly acceptable to have a conversation with my cleavage and call me 'tubs'. 'One day you know Sarah, you might be attractive' he said when I first started. I was sitting in his office whilst he signed his post. He liked the power of making you wait whilst he took phone calls and swivelled in his oversized chair, to accommodate his oversized arse. He bellowed to the whole office last week 'Don't use the loo for a while I'm going for a dump'. All of us know that he's taking this month's issue of 'Women on Top' in with him, so god knows what else we could find in there.

Then there are the others; Robert and Matt, trainee accountants. They work on the top floor. Both complete tossers as well. I used to fancy both of them, not at the same time, but have had my usual crush at some point during my sentence with the firm. Brixham doesn't have an enormous wealth of available man candy so anyone arriving from 'outside the village' is something to be acted on fast, before anyone else bags them.

In the office next to them are Psycho Pete and Bitchy Brenda. Pete does the payroll for our clients and Brenda's the Practice Manager. I've never had it confirmed but I think it's fair to say that Pete has a personality disorder. From one day to the next you never know whether you need to avoid him at all costs and hide all the knives in the kitchen, or if you'll be his best friend and listen to his boring repetitive stories, all of which I've heard before but don't have the guts to say so. Oh and he has a hygiene issue. Dear lord above it's not pleasant. Stomach wrenchingly bad some days if he's stressed. Brenda's just a bitch who likes to pick on me for everything. 'I don't care if it's toilet paper, just photocopy everything that I give you to send' was her rant at me when I first started. She's married with two boys and a husband, Tony, who works for a window company as a fitter. He's half soaked and completely walked over by Brenda. I don't have a lot of confidence but one day I plucked up the courage and stuck up for myself after one of her rants. 'Some people around here couldn't organise a piss up in a brewery,' she said after an invoice hadn't been paid. 'Are you talking about me Brenda? If you are then don't you ever talk to me like that again and get your facts straight'. 'Oh no, Sarah, it wasn't aimed at you, I was just having a rant'. A rant my arse, she was so shocked at my uncharacteristic retaliation, her voice went all funny and sounded like she was having a stroke! I then proceeded to shake back to my desk, as that was the first time I'd ever stuck up for myself.

So that's me. Sarah Banner, early twenties shrivelled up sultana with Diana Ross overly permed red hair. My life, by most standards, is 'run of the mill'. It'll do but I just can't help thinking that I'm destined for something else in this world. I love my home town, don't get me wrong, but I just want to do something else. I think that deep down, I'm outgoing but too afraid to show it and also don't know how to. I'd love to get married and have children, some day, but just not now. It needs to be right because I'm as sure as hell not going to mess it up like my Dad did. But then I met Chris, which marks not only the beginning of my book, but the starting point of my journey to the person I am today, and the beginning of an adventure I never expected to have…

Chapter 1

Meeting Sir Lancelot

I don't wish to be everything to everyone,
but I would like to be something to someone.
Javan

Friday, January, 1998.
Thank God it's Friday. I've never known a week go so blasted
slowly. This year isn't exactly a 'happening' year for me so far.
This place hardly sweeps a single, twenty-something girl off her
feet. The only excitement of today was noticing a new sign on the
main door of the recently converted offices, next to mine. It read
'Williams & Cox, Insurance Brokers', well it shouted the name
really. It was so big it could have been spotted from space. This
could be interesting, new people maybe, who knows. Please
cupid let there be a gorgeous, tall, single, funny, well off, considerate, sultana loving, self-sufficient, sexy man moving in. But the
chances of something like that happening in Brixham? About as
likely as the current Pope renouncing his 'throne', jumping on the
next flight to Tehran to embrace Islam and take on a multitude of
wives.

Monday
Dear fantastic, wonderful, gorgeous Diary, or perhaps I'll just call
you 'Di'! Isn't the world just glorious? After a mundane weekend
of shopping, washing my car and staying in, guess what? I was
just approaching the office when I spotted him – the really tall,
dark and extremely handsome man behind reception. He was so
tall he looked as if he was standing even when seated. Although
not a 'real life' giant, he was about 6ft, 4', and had a big, confident
stride. I know because I watched him stand up and walk off

down the corridor. I physically gasped out loud. I was taken aback by this man, my knight in shining Armani armour! (and somewhere the Pope is eyeing up his first of many wives.)

Cupid, I love you for this and owe you big time. During the morning I made it my mission to pass 'Sir Lancelot's' office as often as possible, notice everything; get all the information I could. My goodness it's not everyday that someone straight out of an Arthurian legend lands on your doorstep... By late afternoon I had plucked up enough courage to actually speak to him, even though I sounded like a Butlins' Redcoat.

'Hello, welcome to Brixham,' I could feel my cheeks glowing red to match my imaginary uniform. It didn't stop me though. I then said, 'Hope you've settled in well.' And yes, still sounding like a Redcoat auditioning for 'Redcoat of the Year'. Oh Di it was painful but I don't think he noticed. He's an insurance broker, which gave me a cunning plan. I calmed down a bit and my imaginary Redcoat just fell off and 'slick, flirty Sarah' kicked in. I told him I was after a quote for my car insurance. I made Chris, as I now know him to be called, laugh, by saying that my current insurers employ a 'pit-ball' for a receptionist, that I daren't ever claim anything in case she actually bites me. He didn't laugh in a *you insane, crazy moron,* way but in a *my, aren't you witty and sweet* way. No idea what happened after that, the rest of that day passed in a blur, I walked around in a lavender haze of bliss.

Tuesday

I took a real interest in what I wore to work today, can't think why really... Decided on a flattering, medium-length skirt (give my legs a bit of an 'airing') instead of my usual boring old 'work trousers'. I coupled it with a brand new red blouse and black tights. Saw Chris and exchanged pleasantries as he uses our office fax. Seeing his face as he walked in made me blush. He really is very sexy. If I was an animal I'd spray my scent on his office door to ward off other prey. Either that or surreptitiously put a 'reserved' sticker on his jacket.

Wednesday, July.

Oh lovely Di, you won't believe what happened today. Sorry not talked to you for a bit, been so preoccupied with how I look, which means a strict regime of preening, shaving and grooming and it's quite hard work, and painful. Anyway, Chris actually asked me out today.

I had 'popped' into his office this morning to ask for something completely unnecessary when he looked up and said, 'Would you like to go to the new Indian for lunch tomorrow?'

Desperately trying to keep my cool, while my legs turned to jelly and my tongue to sandpaper, I managed to get out a rather feeble but well intentioned, 'Yes, that would be great.' This is it; my social life is finally taking off! No longer would I be left on the shelf as one of our clients had so bluntly put it. I'm about to saddle up and ride off into the sunset, well one can dream...

Thursday

I was a waste of space at work today, couldn't settle and dedicated most of my time staring at the clock. Spent twenty minutes in the loo trying to overcome nerves and make sure my hair looked perfect. When 1pm came I sprang up and careful to contain myself, I walked to Chris's office, his colleagues giving me knowing smiles. The restaurant was empty, slightly embarrassing. Chris opted for a Jalfrezi and my first thought was, ooh I could order a Vindaloo, that might impress my new 'love', but back in the real world I would be reduced to a gibbering, perspiring mess, who two hours later would be seen to sprint to the communal office loos more than a dozen times. I opted for a Korma. It was a great date, we laughed a lot. I really like a man who makes me laugh, and Chris continued to tick more of my 'must have' boxes. He paid for lunch and we walked back to the office. Incredibly embarrassing moment as I got my stiletto heel stuck in the bloody pavement. Oh Di I could have died. I had to take the shoe off and prize it out. Chris helped and the up side was that he asked me out again on Saturday evening. I am already going out, but I was quick to invite him over Sunday morning for a coffee.

Sunday

Chris came over, it was lovely. With the house to ourselves, we just talked and talked about everything and anything. I'm so happy as he's asked me out to dinner and I can't wait. I did note his really cute bum and big hands! I really hope that this will go somewhere. I would love to settle down with someone, make a home, have friends over for meals, the usual stuff that couples do. Could Chris be the one who changes my view of men? In other words, that not all of them cheat? Will check in post dinner date. I have lots to do now. I don't have a thing to wear and my hair needs cutting. Wish me luck Di…

Sunday (That was the week that was!)

Good evening Di. I think I'm in love. I have so much to tell you. I spent hours getting ready; bath, shave, body scrub, facial, wash hair. I then got in a panic about what to wear. Half my wardrobe was on the bed, which promptly got chucked on the floor when I got home. Another wonderful evening, though this time the restaurant was packed and I couldn't hear a word Chris was saying, but I tried not to show it; lots of head nodding and smiles.

The sparks began to fly, as we were walking along the promenade looking out to sea. Chris seemed a little shy, so to save myself from internal combustion and perhaps missing the boat altogether, I took the initiative, stopped and leant against the railing and gave him my best 'come hither' look. He got the message, loud and clear, leaned in and kissed me. It was a very special moment. I was swept up in his physical presence, a place that was tender and smelt gorgeous.

And then to top it off, as our lips gently parted, Chris said, 'I've been meaning to kiss you for a long time.' Right there and then, had the ground opened up and swallowed me, I would have died a happy woman with the sound of wedding bells ringing in my ears. Oh Di, this is it, I can just feel it, I could be his Guinevere.

August, September, October and November
One word really – sex. Nothing else of any significance has happened during the last four months. Mind you, if it did, I wouldn't have noticed. Chris and I have been too wrapped up with each other, in more ways than one. Putting it bluntly darling Di, I can hardly walk! It's a good job no one else has access to my diary; I'd just die with the shame. We just can't keep our hands off each other. It's magic and long may it continue. He makes me feel attractive and sexy.

Tuesday, 25th December (Deck the halls with bows of holly, Chris's balls are very jolly!)
First Christmas with my future husband. No, he's not proposed just yet, but he will, trust me. We spent Christmas with Mum and Jayne in Brixham and asked Chris to join us. A huge bag of gifts awaited me; a teddy bear, chocolates, clothes, perfume and underwear (which actually fitted). What a star! Him and Jayne got on well too. Perfect. In the evening Chris and I took a stroll, alone, and he asked me to move in with him! Would you be surprised to hear I said 'yes'? Thought not. Oh Di, 1999 is going to be the best year, I can just feel it.

Tuesday, January, 1999.
Good evening Di. Happy New Year to you! Apologies for not being in touch very much, but I'm a very busy woman now. I moved into Chris's flat last Saturday. It was a bit weird leaving

home, a home I've only ever known, but I can't live there forever. Typical man, Chris hadn't cleared out his wardrobes for my clothes so they're in a heap at the moment in the spare room, along with his bike and TA (Territorial Army) bits. He's at the TA tonight, which is why I've got some time to sit and update you on what's been happening to me. To be honest, the flat needs a damn good clean. Chris is obviously your typical bachelor and it needs a woman's touch. His neighbours don't seem that friendly. The couple underneath can hardly acknowledge me and the lady opposite just gives condescending looks. Weird. Anyway, Mum's coming over and we're going to give the flat a really good clean. Good night Di.

Monday

I'm shattered. I brought Mum over with me on Friday evening as Chris went on a TA weekend straight from work. Our mission was to clean the flat. But in order for you to understand just how much we've done I need to let you know what the place is like. The lounge is basically chipped wood chip wall paper (it's very old), grey carpet and the furniture a 'lovely' sort of 'snotty' olive green colour, including a recliner that if you do try to recline to watch the telly you are thrown back so far it would have been better if it was fixed to the ceiling. The saving grace is the kitchen (but then I'm a girl and I would say that), but it really is! It's a pretty recent addition, imported German units, clean and white with slate coloured work tops, very *über* chic. The spare bedroom is frightening really. It does have a bed in it, but you need a map to find it. Chris certainly needs the ladies' touch. He keeps his bike, TA kit, sports kit, tools and washing in there. I would so love it to be a nice room but will have to pick my moment to bring it up with him.

Anyway, Mum and I set about making it 'nice' (and habitable). We scrubbed, debugged, washed, threw away, laughed, gasped and finally, several hours later, we found ourselves in a clean and quite habitable flat. Adding the new bedding and curtains we bought, it looked a treat. But Chris was not so impressed; in fact he was completely nonplussed when he saw it. Typical man – or is that just him?

Saturday, February.
Chris is away with TA for the weekend so I spent the day cleaning and shopping. Going to cook him a nice meal for when he comes home and run him a lovely hot bath. Oh I'm such a good house 'wife'!

Monday, March.
Just spent hours cuddled up together watching TV with a takeaway and a bottle or two of wine this weekend. Really nice. Chris has busy weeks so likes to make sure he chills out at the weekend and doesn't do much. Very much in love, we spent most of today 'squeezing out' the words 'I love you' and the responses. It's 'our thing'. I squeeze his hand three times, which means 'I love you' and he squeezes mine back four times, which means 'I love you too'. It was bliss.

Thursday
Strange day… Chris received a letter, which made him go very red and blotchy. I've not seen him like that before, and when I asked him what was wrong, he put the letter in his jacket pocket and went to work. When I spoke to him again tonight he just said it was from the bank about an account he was opening and that they just needed some more identification and there was nothing to worry about. I'm not so sure, but he has no reason to lie to me.

Thursday, April.
Erm, hello Di, it has been many weeks since my last entry and during that time I've probably sinned on many occasions! Chris and I have added to our family. No, I'm not pregnant, we have

two kittens. This must mean our relationship is for life if we're getting animals. They're called Smudge and Shanie, two adorable black and white short haired siblings. Love them. I am a very happy girl. Their first day 'home' with us was exhausting; I feel like a new parent. I love my life in this flat. Neighbours are still arsey though and a couple of Chris's TA friends came over the other Saturday to drop something off and I'm sure they smirked at me. When I told Chris about it, he just shrugged it off.

Saturday, May.
Chris is away with the TA again this weekend, so I got up late, went shopping, ate chocolate and watched soppy old movies. Will spend most of tomorrow getting the place tidy and cook Chris's favourite roast dinner ready for when he comes home. This is the life, mind you I must catch up with my friends. I feel I've been so involved with moving in with Chris and settling down, that I've forgotten the outside world. I feel terribly serious and grown up now!

Chapter 2

The Wedding

If love is blind, marriage is the eye-opener.
Coolnsmart.com

Tuesday, June.
I'm in a couple now and with two cats to think about, some days I don't have time to fart. Chris is working long hours and is now away with the TA every other weekend, so I spend a lot of time cleaning and shopping and before you know it the weekend has gone. I do get bored sometimes though and miss being able to pop in to see friends. Plymouth isn't miles away from Brixham, but I'm just so busy working, cleaning, cooking and making sure Chris is okay. Anyway, can't remember everything that's gone on since I last spoke to you, but suffice to say things really are moving in the right direction. House-hunting has been the main thing, moving nearer to where we work. Chris still works in Brixham, but thankfully, I left 'Toss on' a while ago and got another job in Torquay. He suffered a stroke and sold the business to another accountant who had an office in Torquay. I put it down to too much porn. Found a lovely little place, and no need for a bleaching top to bottom this time either. And the sound of wedding bells are getting louder (well in my head anyway). Yes, this year really is shaping up to be something quite special.

Monday (Wedding Gate)
I've had *the* most sickening weekend ever in my life so far. I was tidying out a cupboard in the lounge. Some would say I was being nosey, but I like to think of it as being methodical. Anyway, there it was, with the words 'Our Wedding' written in black

marker pen, on the spine of a video, sat innocently in the middle of 'Rambo' and 'X Files'. It just flew at me in a way I just couldn't avoid. I went all hot and felt a bit sick. Part of me thought, 'Don't you dare watch it Sarah, it's a private family video, probably his brother's wedding. Chris will show you it one day.' The other part of me, the part I tend to listen to more on occasions like this, thought, 'Bollocks, what are you waiting for woman, put it on!'

So I did. I have no idea how long it went on for, but it was like I'd been watching it for days. I was aware of my surroundings but felt I was having an out of body experience, because I couldn't actually believe what I was watching. I was waiting for Chris to do a piece to camera and tell me off for being nosey, but he didn't. He did speak, but it wasn't to me. It was to a pretty girl called Rachel. What were those words again, oh yes, I do. Two simple, matter of fact words that we all say in everyday conversations, except that, on this occasion, these two simple words meant a bond, a pact between two people, for life. I rushed to the toilet and threw up. I was too stunned to cry and tortured myself by watching more. I don't know what I hoped to gain by doing this. Maybe it was to find a piece of evidence to reassure me that Chris was the best man and I'd got it wrong. But when I watched the 'first dance' with the two of them dancing very closely together, I realised that my search for reassurance was futile.

It was 9.00pm when I finished watching. I suddenly became aware that the only light in the flat was coming from the television. I'd been watching my life turn upside down for five hours. I managed to gather myself together and sort myself out. It was then I had a flashback to the letter Chris received about three months ago. I needed to find it. It took me half an hour of turning the place upside down but I found it stuffed in a sock in his underwear drawer. It was from her solicitor, filing for divorce on the grounds of adultery – with me. Suddenly, I understood why the neighbours weren't friendly. Why I don't go to any TA do's. It's not because I don't know anyone and will be bored, it's because someone will mention his bloody wife! By midnight, the shock had subsided a bit and I cried and cried. When I looked at the clock in the bedroom it was 3.40am. I cried myself to sleep and woke up feeling crap at 9.30am. Chris was due home at about 2.00pm. I was going to cook him a roast and lemon meringue pie but I felt like I'd got the flu and couldn't get out of bed. Sorry to go on Di, but I just need to get all of this down on paper and can't face telling Mum that I've potentially messed things up.

Today is Monday and I'm still in shock. Chris came home at 3.00pm covered in crap from having slept in a field. He took one look at me and thought someone had died, as my eyes were hardly visible through continual crying. I'd composed myself a bit and just handed him the solicitor's letter and the video. He went grey within seconds and all he could mutter was, 'I'm so sorry.' We spent hours talking. He opened up to me about how the marriage was over when they moved to Plymouth from Bristol and they relocated for a fresh start. She'd apparently had lots of affairs and the latest one he'd found out about was the last straw. He didn't wear a ring because in his eyes the marriage died a long time ago. His reason for not telling me about it was pure embarrassment at being divorced by twenty six and the fact that his wife had been unfaithful. I asked him why the neighbours were so off with me when she'd moved out long before I came on the scene. Apparently he'd been sleeping in the spare bedroom for months but the neighbours didn't know. But I do love him and feel sorry for him. It can't have been easy.

Thursday

Had the biggest bouquet of red roses delivered to the office on Tuesday, with the words I love you on the card. Bless him; they must have cost a fortune. Mum not quite so pleased but is willing to give Chris another chance. She can partly see his reasons, but we've been so used to the men in our lives lying to us that we almost expect it I guess. I'll be fine. I'll get over it. We chatted more on Tuesday night and last night. Chris said that Rachel used to belittle him in public and he apparently got on her nerves. She said he was selfish and intolerant which I don't believe. He's very generous and attentive. If anything, I'm intolerant and I can see him trying not to shout at me sometimes; I like the heating on and he doesn't, so I try and tolerate the cold. I hate sport on the TV, he loves it, so I'm putting up with it now. I love to get up early at the weekends now as I hate wasting the day, but Chris likes to lie in so I'm trying to be tolerant and think of his needs too.

Wednesday, July (Two weeks after Wedding Gate)
We seemed to have turned a corner and we've found a house in Torquay. I'm so excited. We should exchange within the next week or so and complete two weeks after that. Both of us need a fresh start. I know Chris needs to get rid of the reminders of this flat and the unhappiness Rachel caused.

Tuesday, August.
We're in our new house! So lovely to close the door on the flat and all the ghosts and bad memories it held. We moved in last Friday and I just sat in our new lounge, propped up against the wall, waiting for the removal van to arrive, surveying my first ever house. I was so happy, I cried. I'm 'grown-up' at last. This is where I'm going to have my 2.4 children, a rose bush and a picket fence! It even felt as if the house was excited for me and our new neighbours, Barbara and Neil, seem lovely and told us to just ask if we need anything. Chris' divorce has come through too which is great news. He's definitely all mine now!

Friday (Two weeks being a home owner!)
Bloody TA! (So cross today, I've renamed them the 'Territorial Arseholes'). Whenever I need help from Chris, there's always something going on with that bloody lot. I know he's moved

units and wants to impress, but he's away again now until Sunday afternoon and has left me to deal with the decorators. I know the money's good but it's supposed to be a hobby, not a bloody lifestyle. I thought with us moving into our own proper home, Chris would want to be with me more and make time to make the house look nice. Have I changed? Has he changed? Or are my rose coloured spectacles losing their tint? Perhaps I need to go to the opticians, or maybe just the off license...

Wednesday, September.

Where has the time gone? My, what a busy summer this has been; endless barbeques, spending hours eating and drinking with friends, just living for the moment. Getting to work takes literally ten minutes instead of an hour and we are both less stressed. When Chris is away with TA I either garden or do the shopping and housework, and just enjoy being a sensible home owner. I like to look after him too and whilst, sometimes, he works late, plays rugby twice a week and has TA commitments, which really do get on my nerves, I knew he had these hobbies when I met him so I can't complain. My old hobbies of squash and aerobics seem to have been forgotten. The house seems huge compared to the little flat we had, plus I have a garden to sort out. If I relied on Chris to cut the grass for me, you wouldn't be able to see the house at all.

October

We're engaged! Oh my God I can't believe it. I chose the ring months ago and told Chris which one it was. No surprises but at least it's the one I want. It's gold with three diamonds. Chris took me to a rock on our favourite beach in Brixham and proposed. I knew he was going to do it as I could see the box bulging out of his coat pocket, not quite how I'd dreamed as he's not very demonstrative unfortunately but it's the sentiment that counts I suppose. I broached the marriage subject with him shortly after the divorce came through. He's told me endless times how he wants to spend the rest of his life with me as I apparently 'complete him'. I phoned everyone and anyone I could and told them. Mum and Jayne cried and can't wait for the wedding!

Friday, December.

I'm going to be Mrs Sarah Chilton on Saturday 18th November next year! My stomach churns with excitement just thinking about it. I've started thinking about wedding dresses today. I've always fancied an off-the-shoulder number, ivory, long veil and trane and a bouquet of red roses. I sat for about an hour today listening to Chicago's I am a man who will fight for your honour. I imagined myself walking down the aisle in church and everyone gasping and saying how beautiful I look. I really need to stop being so vain! As Chris has been married before, it's been difficult to find a vicar to marry us. I tried a couple, but they weren't very receptive. Chris's Godmother lives in the New Forest and when we went to see her a couple of weeks ago she came up with the idea that we get married there.

There's a lovely Manor House, called The *New Hampshire Manor*, which has just received its wedding licence. On our first visit there was a touch of frost still in the air, newly settled on the grounds and deer roaming around without a care in the world and the drive up to the Manor House was breathtaking. The imposing gates gave you just a hint of the property. It stood tall and proud as if blowing out its chest, showing off its stately attributes. It's just perfect. Stained glass windows, two big open fire places in the reception and lounge area and an air of tranquillity. And the ceremonial room was lovely – nice and big too, so plenty of room for our guests. I cannot contain myself. I am like a child waiting for Christmas morning whilst knowing it's only March. I was a bit cross with Chris though. He'd been out with friends the night before and was hung-over and couldn't have cared less if we'd been to visit a slaughter house as a potential venue. God, men can be so insensitive...

Saturday, March, 2000.
I need to invent another word for stress. I am beyond stress. Stress is down at the bottom of 'Mood Mountain' and I'm at the peak, the very pointy top bit. I'm doing most of the organising; all Chris has done is stipulate that he'd like an exotic honeymoon as his first one was in the UK. We went to the travel agents at the weekend and booked a fortnight in the Maldives. We've also booked a night on our own 'Robinson Crusoe' Island. It's going to be just us for the whole night, doing what most honeymooners do, I guess... I'm very excited about that! Not so excited about the price mind you. We've had to put it on the credit card. I know Chris wanted something special this time, but we could have gone to Rome, which is where I fancied. It's so romantic there, and the love capital of the world let's face it and I fancied sipping champagne in St Mark's Square, whilst holding hands with my new husband. Never mind, he's happy.

Saturday, April.
Went wedding dress shopping with Mum today and tried on piles of wedding dresses, some just for a laugh! So many literally made me skip and sing 'fiddle de diddle de dee' because they were so puffy and full and I did have concerns that I may not actually be able to get through the door of the ceremonial room in the hotel! The shop assistants weren't impressed, but Mum and I found it funny. Puffy meringue dresses just aren't me. I really don't suit satin and just couldn't find any that suited me. So, I've ended up settling for a very dark green bridesmaid's dress of all things. Short sleeved with velvet at the top and silk at the bottom. It's lovely, but I wish I could have found the one in my dreams. Never mind.

Tuesday, December.

Oh wow, I'm Mrs Chilton! I'm a married woman with a wedding ring on to prove it. It's going to take ages to write everything down that's happened over the last few weeks, but I shall start from the very beginning and write it properly so that I can read it in years to come. The day I had dreamed about since I was a child was actually here. I went and had my hair and makeup done and felt a million dollars. Everyone in the hairdressers was looking at me and I liked to think they were jealous of me, knowing who I was going to marry and wishing it could be them. Does every bride think this or is just me?

The weather was still lovely. We were very lucky because the night before it rained all evening and I was praying it would stop. There was an air of excitement all around and I was beaming, positively radioactive! Chris had sent some champagne for breakfast and I felt wonderful and slightly tipsy actually. Everyone had arrived at the hotel and Mum and I were driving to it over the New Forest or 'Black Forest' as she referred to it when she announced, 'I love the Black Forest, especially at this time of the year'.

'I'm sure it's lovely Mum, but as we're in the New Forest, I couldn't possibly comment on the Black Forest!' I think that was her eighteenth faux pas of the year, her seventeenth being that she wouldn't like to go skiing but would enjoy the afro skiing afterwards.

Waiting to walk into the ceremonial room where I was to become Mrs Chilton was so nerve racking. I knew Chris was in there waiting for me and I hoped I looked lovely for him. Mum was nervous too as she was giving me away. She deserved to, she'd been a Mum and Dad to me since I was eight and Dad left us, and it was her privilege to do this. The words 'we're ready for you now' made my stomach scream with nerves once more. All eyes were on me and I can remember swinging Mum's arm as we walked down the aisle. Why I did this is beyond me, pure nerves

I guess, but it was quite a prominent swing and I felt I should have sung 'ring a ring of roses' and skipped. Never mind, it's done now. Chris looked great and I felt so proud to be having him as my husband. He said his vows so loudly and with such conviction I nearly cried again. I've never had a man love me this much. After all, I was the sultana who thought she'd never find love. We kissed as 'Mr and Mrs' and everyone came up and congratulated us. We had the compulsory photo session and then went to the hotel for the celebrations. It was the hotel Chris and I stayed in whilst looking at venues. Very friendly and the right size for us. The New Hampshire Manor was a bit too expensive unfortunately. If we hadn't spent so much on the honeymoon I think we could have managed the reception there but I didn't dare mention that to Chris as he always said Rachel was controlling and bossy and I don't want to end up like her.

Poor Chris, he's not a great speaker. I don't think he'd prepared anything, as he wasn't using any notes, just speaking 'off the cuff'. It wasn't good and I was slightly embarrassed, for him mainly. He thanked everyone for coming at least three times, whilst nervously rubbing his hands together, and did the compulsory toasts. I have to admit to being slightly put out as, having watched his first attempt one fateful Saturday afternoon, it was a lot better than this. When I plucked up courage to look at my family and friends, I could see the look of embarrassment on their faces. The food was lovely and everyone seemed to enjoy themselves. All in all I had a fabulous day. It went too quickly though. I went to bed before Chris, as I was so tired, hoping he'd follow, but he came up drunk about three hours later. We didn't consummate our marriage that night. Can you believe it? Everyone expects the wedding night to be full of sex, sex and more sex with some sex thrown in! We didn't even do it the next day as Chris was hung over. Oh well, we had the exotic honeymoon to look forward to. On the Sunday we jetted off to the

Maldives. It was an eleven hour flight, which was spent sat apart in order that Chris had enough leg room. I complained and told the stewardess that we were on honeymoon, but no one moved. Chris didn't kick up a fuss so I decided to shut up. Not a great start, sitting in a different seat from your new husband. I was sat with another newly wed couple and could see Chris in the row in front of me just reading his book. When we arrived in the capital city of Male, the weather was really rough so we were forced to ride it out in a rather basic hotel on the mainland. Luckily, the next morning the weather was much better and we got a boat to the water plane base. The flight over was just wonderful. The sea was aqua marine, so calm with a few remote islands dotted here and there. I was so excited about seeing what our island looked like.

We received a lovely welcome. The staff were playing music for the guests and we were given garlands. It was like being in Hawaii! The novel thing about our room, which was more like a little bungalow to be honest, was the outdoor bathroom. I felt so strange peeing outside. No one could see us as there was a wall hiding us. The shower area was huge and so I was anticipating having a good time in this area over the next couple of weeks.

Unfortunately, the romance didn't go quite according to plan. We were allotted seats in the restaurant and so had to sit with the same couple for the whole two week period. Darren and Helen were a nice enough couple, but I wanted romance; walks along the beach, and sunset kisses, but it didn't happen. Chris had always wanted to learn how to dive and where better to learn than the Indian Ocean. It was expensive to be honest and I thought we'd spent enough on the wedding and put too much on the credit card, but I didn't like to see the look of disappointment on his face when I said this so gave in and reluctantly, but dutifully, agreed he should do it. So he signed up for a seven day PADI diving course, which included a night dive.

Chris was happy and it was nice to see him enjoying this

honeymoon considering his last one was such a disaster, apparently. Luckily, I made a friend, Sam. Her boyfriend, Tim, was on the same course as Chris and so we spent our days together on the beach and having lunch together. She was a lovely girl and it was great to relax, but I wanted to do it with my new husband. And I don't even want to mention the Robinson Crusoe deserted island 'experience'. It didn't happen. We were talking to a couple that had done it a couple of days before us and they told us that fishermen would come on the beach during the night and she had got bitten to death by mosquitoes. There wasn't enough food or drink and the tent they were given to sleep in left a lot to be desired so we cancelled the trip.

I felt a bit deflated to be honest coming home. I wasn't feeling that I'd spent a holiday on cloud nine with my fabulous new husband having sex for breakfast lunch and dinner and just going for food to get energy for the next sex session. We didn't even have sex on honeymoon. The only cardiovascular exercise I had was aerobic sessions whilst on my own. Chris was either out diving or hung over from drinking in the free bar with Tim and some other people we'd met, the night before. We came home to a credit card bill for the wedding, honeymoon and an expensive diving course on top of it. Chris and I had a row because he had the nerve to comment on the £30 necklace I'd bought myself at duty free. I shouldn't be feeling like this, should I?

Chapter 3

Wanting a Baby

Making a decision to have a child...it's momentous. It is to decide forever to have your heart go walking around outside your body.
Elizabeth Stone

Sunday, March, 2002.

I have to admit to being a bit bored, in fact, so much so that I haven't even found anything noteworthy to write about for over a year. Months and months have just crawled past; getting up, working, coming home, cleaning, cooking, shopping and ironing and going to bed. I really hoped the honeymoon was the low point and that things would pick up again. What's happened? I used to love sex with my first love, Craig. Chris and I always have a hug and a kiss, but just don't do it much. Should this worry me? Friends say that it's normal and other things take over. Chris is either working late, playing rugby or away with the TA so we don't get a lot of time for us. And he's not very spontaneous. I tend to initiate sex and it's not bad when it happens but I wish he'd take charge sometimes. Does he not know by now that women can't orgasm to order? We've talked about having a family; maybe this will get us going!

Saturday, May.

Chris and I have decided to have a baby. We're happy, content and ready. I'm late twenties, and don't want to wait forever. We went to the doctors today to have my coil removed, I really did not relish the thought of my male doctor visiting my 'lady garden'. It's just not right in my opinion, having someone else 'fiddle' with your bits, poke around and pull out the coil is like he's having a go in a tombola. Last night, we had some nice food, bottle of wine and had sex and then thought, 'Oh my God what have we done?' Not in a regretful way, but in an exciting way, as we may have just made a baby! It's woken us both up sexually too as we just keep having sex now. I think we'd both got ourselves into a routine of work, looking after a house and all the issues that ensue from this.

Thursday, August

Oh bloody hell, I'm three days late. I'm always on time. Could this be it? I've decided not to tell Chris yet, he seems preoccupied at the moment. He's busy at work and going away on a lot of courses, plus TA weekends. I'm going to buy a pregnancy kit tomorrow and do a test on my own. Wish me luck!

Mum to be Monday

I'm going to be a Mum! I'm pregnant! Chris was at work and I did the test at home on my own first thing this morning. Weeing on a stick isn't pleasant I have to say. I was shaking with excitement, trepidation, and panic. It was such a special moment and I wish he'd been there really as I didn't envisage being on my own at this point and I feel a bit deflated, but Chris is worried about something and I didn't want to disappoint him just in case it transpired I wasn't pregnant. He would have been really upset and I would have felt I'd let him down. I phoned him straight away… 'How do you fancy being a Dad?' I obviously caught him unawares because he sounded quite shocked.

Bless him, all he said was, 'You're pregnant?' He didn't sound as excited as I would have liked. I'd planned this moment in my head for years. The moment you tell your husband that you're about to have his baby should be followed by fireworks, champagne corks popping and him crying and saying how happy you've made him and how complete he feels. Instead, all I got was 'You're pregnant?' I hope he's okay. I keep asking him and he's told me he's fine and that work is getting him a bit stressed as they've just taken over another firm up country and so he's been helping set that up. I phoned Mum and her reaction was a lot better than Chris's. She cried and told me she was proud of me. Jayne phoned me too and said the same. Chris came home with a bottle of bubbly and a dozen red roses. Bit disappointed as they were supermarket ones (bought in a hurry, out of duty is how I felt). We sat and talked about things and I only had a small glass of champagne. I'm pregnant now and have something growing inside me. I need to be responsible and sensible.

Wednesday
I reckon I'm twelve weeks pregnant. I have a midwife, Jenny. She's okay. She's not had children though and is a little impatient and quite matronly for someone in her thirties. I don't feel us bonding. I'm seeing her tomorrow for a scan. Tummy feeling a bit swollen and the button on my work trousers won't do up at all! It's so weird!

Thursday
I'm crying writing this. What a bloody awful day I had yesterday. I went for a twelve week scan at the doctors. I was so excited as I wanted to hear the heartbeat. Chris was busy so couldn't come unfortunately. The silence was deafening, no heartbeat. Jenny took ages to scan my tummy trying to find one. She said that sometimes the baby hides which is why you can't find one, but then after what seemed like hours, she said the words, 'I'm going to send you up to the hospital as I can't hear a heartbeat.' She may as well have said 'I don't think the baby's alive and we need to check'. I was in a right state and started crying. I phoned Chris who left work and met me at the hospital. He didn't sound worried, but I know he was trying to reassure me.

We made our way to the maternity section, but it was very quiet up there. I felt I was in the 'you've lost your baby' section as everyone looked pensive and seemed to give me 'I'm so sorry for your loss' looks. We waited in a room for what seemed like hours and sat under the window. The weather was gloriously hot and Chris and I decided that if the baby was dead, it was meant to be and there was nothing we could do about it. We'd try again. This happens to women all the time and my heart goes out to them right now, because writing this I feel the luckiest woman in the world. A stern looking lady walked in and told me to lie on the bed. She didn't reassure me one bit and I felt a bit of an incon-venience. I was an emergency appointment and she had other things she should be doing. All I kept focussing on was the massive blackhead she had on her neck. I felt sick just being there so that crater didn't make me feel any better.

She bluntly said, 'I just can't find a heartbeat,' in a way that was so natural for her she could have been out shopping, announcing to her girlfriend that she couldn't find the right cereal (she was obviously gay, no man would have fancied that mountain growing on her neck). I had so many sarcastic and blunt things to say to her about her attitude and growth i.e. are you growing that for charity and does it have heartbeat? but kept quiet as I was getting myself so upset. Then suddenly I heard it, very faint and extremely fast, but it was there, my baby's heartbeat, reassuring me and telling me not to give up on it yet. I started to cry. I'm apparently four weeks ahead in my dates so I'm only eight weeks pregnant and not twelve, hence the reason for not being able to find a heartbeat so easily. I cried a lot yesterday afternoon. I know it was relief and a release of built up tension. God bless all women who have had a miscarriage.

Saturday, October.
Extension started today. Bit of a bugger really because we never thought I'd get pregnant so quickly. We should have postponed it as soon as we knew, the builders were friendly and so would have understood, but Chris, however, decided we should go ahead and to think of the equity it would give us in the house.

Why that was relevant I have no idea. We are hardly likely to sell up after extending, no way! We had looked at moving but there was nothing around that we liked so opted for an extension. Barbara and Neil have had one done and it looks amazing. Anyway, the digger arrived to dig up foundations and knock down a wall in the garden. Not impressed with Chris – away yet again with the TA. I did remind him that he's not the only medic, but apparently he had no choice to go. I was left to deal with the builders and run around making coffee and bacon sandwiches all day. I'm not confident enough to deal with any problems they may present me with. I don't like male dominated environments and Chris should have been here. The forklift truck knocked over Barbara and Neil's wall and I got myself really stressed. Chris had better love the roast I've also made and not say a bloody word. I wish I'd put my foot down with him and told him to postpone the bloody thing but I can't be doing with the hassle.

Monday, December.
Really enjoying my pregnancy now. Whilst I felt sick at the beginning, luckily I never was. Ginger biscuits helped so much. Bought some new maternity clothes at the weekend and I feel properly pregnant now. People are patting my tummy and asking me lots of questions. Going to go shopping for the pram soon. I want a traditional one, just like in 'Mary Poppins'! I've been preparing myself for what lays ahead of me i.e. buying nappies, wipes, baby grows, cot, gorgeous cream bedding with little bears embossed on it. I'm reading endless magazines, which tell me the size of the baby and how it's developing. What exercises I can do, with baby, to get fit again after its born. One channel on the television is devoted to maternity stuff and births, so I've watched a lot of them too. Whilst it all looks painful, we see the parents at home a couple of weeks later and the mum looks well and really happy so I can't wait for that.

Tuesday
Had a scan today and it was absolutely amazing. Actually seeing your baby is incredible, even in a blurry black and white bubble! He was sucking his thumb. (Not that we know it's a boy, I want a surprise.) Hearing the heartbeat again is just so reassuring and I feel really special knowing that I'm growing another human being.

Wednesday
Took the scan photo to work today and have now put it up next to my computer. Chris said he knew what he looked like in his head so I could have the photo to do with as I wished. I feel so proud and can't stop looking at it. I'm sure the hospital have figured out a way of making money from the scans by just printing out the same one as all scan photos look the same to me!

Friday, February, 2003.
I'm officially on maternity leave now! Thank God. I'm shattered. I'm sure there's more than one in here, either that or baby has come armed with his own suitcase of necessities. It's nice to think that I don't have to go to work now for a few months. It's Valentine's Day and you're probably wondering Di why I'm spending the evening with you instead of having a romantic dinner with Chris? Well, although the extension is finished, there is still a lot of painting to be done and so Chris spent the evening finishing off the fourth bedroom. Get me, fourth bedroom! I told him to relax and I'd order a takeaway but he wants to get the painting finished. He's obviously still got a lot on his mind at the moment with work, so I'm going to do my bit by helping to paint the nursery and a couple of doors. Chris is away for a couple of nights next week working in the new branch 'up north' so I'll surprise him with my painting skills when he comes home. I have sciatica quite badly at the moment and it's helpful being on all fours for some reason, so I spent the morning cleaning the dust

and crap off the wooden floor in the lounge. Chris hasn't got time to do it at the moment what with work and going away so I'm adopting the attitude that I'm only pregnant and not disabled. I think he appreciates what I'm doing; he's not a man of many words.

Wobbly Wednesday, April.
I swear to anything that will listen, if this baby doesn't arrive soon I'm going to go stark raving mad. I have developed a proper pregnancy waddle and look like I've soiled myself quite frankly. I squelch when I walk due to the water in my ankles, which are now the size of my thighs. I'm hot, fed up, tired, and feel like Violet Beauregarde from Charlie and the sodding Chocolate Factory. I shall be rolled to hospital if I get any bigger. If anyone else says to me 'My you look fit to drop any second' I'll swing for them. One friend of Mum's said 'still not had it then?' In my head I replied 'Yes, I had it yesterday but missed my bump so much I decided to shove a stuffed animal up there for effect'. In reality I didn't need to say anything as my face obviously spoke a thousand words and my reply was obvious by its silence! Not happy today, can you tell?

Saturday
Today is my due date. Ankles are now the size of my stomach. I have to sit like a fat man with legs splayed out and tummy protruding. All femininity has flown out of the window. Jenny the 'ice' midwife came today and when I asked to be induced she just said, and I'm sure she smirked at this point, but maybe paranoia setting in, 'We'll review the situation in a couple of days'. Bitch – I'm going mad and want the bloody thing out now...

Monday
'Ice Jenny' actually showed some compassion today and I am

going in to hospital to be induced today. I'm so relieved, nervous and excited too. I know that the next time I set foot in this house I'll be bringing my son or daughter home. What a very exciting thought. Will catch up as soon as I can and fill you in with all my news... Wish me luck!

Wednesday, May (Post Natal Disaster)
Oh well Di, here goes. I was induced at 9.30am on the 15th of April and it was then a case of waiting to see what happened. The ward was quiet and so I was lucky enough to have my own room. I was so bored and restless. Giving birth doesn't happen every day so I couldn't settle. Chris sat there and read his book and was in his own little world. I couldn't relax because I could break my waters at any time and it would be all hands on deck. I found it all a bit daunting really and wanted Chris to hold my hand and reassure me that everything would be fine. I told him I was bored and a bit worried and he told me to read too. Not much help.

We had a walk around the block and a few hours later Mum and Jayne arrived. Jayne just made me laugh. They'd been to Marks & Spencer before coming to visit me and, Mum being Mum, decided to try and ascend the escalator on the coming down one whilst shouting 'Oh shit oh bloody hell Jayne'. Apparently, the whole shop was in stitches! A midwife came in to see if I was all right and asked if I'd eaten. I hadn't even thought of food to be honest and had just sat staring out of the window waiting for my waters to break for most of the day. My mind was trying to recall the antenatal classes, but I really couldn't remember anything they taught us at all. I wish Chris had been to some as he may have remembered something. They always fell on a bloody TA or rugby night. I remember being told about pain relief, having a tour of the maternity unit, and what happens if baby is still born. Fab, not much help to me now.

Anyway, by this time I was actually hungry and fancied something light. The kitchen was closed apparently but the midwife said she would see what she could do for me. I can remember Jayne, Mum and I laughing when the she came in with the food. Someone had obviously given birth shortly before because she presented me with what can only be described as heated up placenta. I think, but this was never confirmed, it was cheesy bolognaise all minced up. It was food so I just got on with it. We laughed so much that evening, it did me good and took my mind off the fact that I was about to endure labour any time soon and push a square peg out of a round hole. Up until now labour was something I'd deal with and get on with. Billions of women do it and cope, but I had a sudden feeling of 'there's no going back now Sarah' and I felt a little scared. I wish I'd been a bit more mentally prepared for this because in a few hours time it was no longer going to be Chris and Sarah, but Chris, Sarah and baby. I'm going to have responsibilities and a human being wholeheartedly dependent on me

Everyone had left by 10pm. I was just going to the loo at about 10.30pm I think it was, before getting some sleep when I coughed and fluid ran down my leg. Well, this is it, it's started. Poor Chris, when the midwife rang he was just getting into bed. It was deathly quiet on the delivery suite, which was shattered every so often by blood curdling screams of someone actually giving birth (I hoped anyway). It was 3am and the moon was shining into my room. I felt protected by it, as if it wanted to keep an eye on me and keep me company as Chris was still reading his book. It was very peaceful. At 5am a midwife asked if I'd like a bath, which sounded a very good idea. Chris sat on the chair by the bath and we just talked, knowing it was going to be our last time for a long, long time to talk on our own without being interrupted by our child. It was a very special time for me as Chris was so attentive and I felt very close to him. It's at times like this you realise just what's ahead of you. We're not prepared mentally for this, it's all about the physical preparations; cot, diet, nursery, pram, maternity leave etc, but no one prepares you psychologically for it and I'm writing this with the benefit of hindsight. My expectations of a two to three hour labour, natural birth, skin-to-skin and immediate bonding, just as I'd seen on the birthing programmes, sure as hell didn't live up to the reality.

That evening I just wanted the darned thing out. I'd seen a complete turn around of midwives; Jenny was surprised to see me again but if she'd said anything sarcastic I would have thrown my pan of newly regurgitated blackcurrant juice and chicken salad sandwich at her. Eventually the doctors decided on a C-section. One of them was Italian and I couldn't understand a word he said. I didn't care by this point to be honest and just nodded in what I hoped were the right places. He'd had a good old look 'down there' so many times during the day and actually asked if he could bring some students in to show them how to break waters. By this time I'd lost all pride and dignity and asked if he wanted to bring the bin men in as well whilst he was at it.

At 12.30am on the 17th of April, I was wheeled down to the operating theatre. At 1.12am Johnathan Albert James Chilton was born. I awoke to a midwife telling me, 'Sarah, you've got a boy.' Then waking again, mid-morning back in my own room. Johnathan was next to me in the cot asleep. I was numb. What on earth had I just been through and who the hell was this? 'Excuse me, someone's left a baby by my bed, could you take it away please?' I want tea, toast and someone to talk to. When you start a new job, no one expects you to know everything from the word go. You're broken in gently and given time to adapt to your new career, but I felt like I'd hit the ground running – quite tough after a C-section. I was on my own with Johnathan and couldn't even sit up, let alone feed him. I was so tired too and felt panic stricken. I had no idea what to do and just wanted to sleep and process what I'd been through. The whole world needed to sod off for a bit and leave me to my thoughts.

Friday

Didn't leave my room as I just couldn't face anyone and was still numb from the anaesthetic and epidural. Chris had to change Johnathan's nappy as I'm too tired and, quite frankly, scared. I had three midwives around me today trying to teach me how to breastfeed. I couldn't take to it at all, it was painful beyond words. I was constantly sweating and shivering, but I wanted to stick with it. They were round the bed grabbing my boobs and squeezing my nipples to help Johnathan latch on. One of them was a French lady, who was very old school. I wanted to tap her on the shoulder (no, that's a lie, I wanted to punch her really hard actually) and say, 'Oi, these boobs don't come off you know, funnily enough I'm actually attached to them but if you carry on doing what you're doing 'Madame' your head wont be attached to your body.'

Johnathan was just shoved on and that was my introductory lesson in breastfeeding over and done with. Great, thanks for that ladies. I just wanted a couple of days to myself to process what I'd been through and have a lot of sleep. He's not latching on well and keeps crying and making a clicking noise but French Mafia Midwife keeps telling me I'm doing it wrong. Anyway hunger and dehydration got the better of me and I decided to venture out onto the ward for breakfast. I could barely walk and didn't want to draw attention to myself. Why were other Mums looking happy and laughing? How come they were walking normally and wearing clothes? What had I missed out on? What had I not done right?

One of the midwives looked at me on the way back and gasped at me with shock (not very reassuring). She told me I looked dreadful (you don't say) and thought I was anaemic. Despite telling her several times that I was fine, she insisted on getting a doctor to see me as she thought I needed a blood transfusion. I didn't stop and protest and just shuffled back to my room. I looked in the mirror to see what all the fuss was about. I hadn't looked at myself since Tuesday morning when I looked relatively normal. Who was the woman looking back at me? I had no idea who she was. Where had Sarah gone? I looked behind me convinced that there was someone else in the room because this person wasn't me. All I could see was dishevelled, greasy hair, a frighteningly white pallor and eyes that looked not only tired and puffy, but also overwhelmingly sad and frightened. I looked like I'd witnessed first hand some terrible atrocities and was still getting over the experience. I examined every inch of my face with my dead eyes whilst leaning against the sink in my room. This wasn't me, yet the person in the mirror had tears falling down her cheeks too. She looked how I felt, numb, shocked, empty, and so, so disappointed. Just after lunch on day two of being a Mum, one of the duty doctors came to see me and said that I desperately needed a blood transfusion as I was anaemic and had lost a lot of blood during the caesarean. He said I could have it in tablet form, but it would take longer to get into my system, perhaps two to three days, and so he suggested I had a blood transfusion straightaway. I just wanted to get better and so opted for the transfusion. So there I lay, linked up to a prop from Dr Who – a tall, metal pole on wheels with a bag of blood hanging from it, receiving units of someone else's blood. The whole thing felt yucky. Weird, because I give blood, but to receive it just didn't feel right. I started to feel better a few hours later and by the next day I felt a lot better. The midwife in charge came to see me and I put on my happiest face and tried to look as if giving birth was one of my hobbies.

Saturday

The time in hospital was a blur. I felt numb and empty. If I'd had the energy I'd have been on my knees, pleading to go home, but I didn't think I'd be able to get up again. I wanted to surround myself with familiar things; my family, my bedroom, the cats – things that made me happy and took me back to a place where I

knew happiness and peace. I hadn't showered since Johnathan
was born and I just wanted to be clean again and put some make
up on and look and feel like me. At least if I looked like me,
people would think I was alright and enjoying being a Mum and
no one would bother me with questions like 'Are you okay,
Sarah? You look tired and fed up.' I didn't want to speak to the
other new Mums, who were happy, as it would just remind me
just how shit I felt. The duty midwife came and asked why I felt
the need to go home so soon. She felt I should stay in for a bit
longer because I'd just had a blood transfusion. I told her it was
because my Sister was going home soon and I wanted to get
back to normal family life. She looked at me for any signs of a
crack and then said she'd review the situation again in the
morning. I was too tired to feel excited and couldn't wait to prise
these mesh pants off me. They'd been on for what seemed like
an age and I was worried they'd leave permanent marks in my
skin.

Sunday
Chris came in and handed all the midwives the obligatory tin of
chocolates and biscuits, whilst I was getting ready. I'd had a
shower earlier on and put on normal pants. It was like being
released from prison. I was leaving my cell in my own clothes
and discarding anything that was prison issue. I had make-up
on and had done my hair. Johnathan was wearing the 'going
home from hospital outfit' that Chris insisted on buying him. It
was a pair of apple green cord dungarees with white baby grow
underneath and matching green hat. He looked so sweet and a
little funny; the hat was a bit big and it kept falling over his face,
so he resembled a tennis ball in dungarees. I didn't say many
goodbyes, as I was worried the midwives would see the look of
shock on my face and make me stay in this 'House of Disaster'.
Chris carried the car seat and we left the hospital with our son.
I put on my I'm so happy and feel a mature and sensible Mum

look. In reality I was so exhausted and just wanted to get home. I waited in the lobby whilst Chris went and got the car. We both panicked a bit as Johnathan's head kept flopping about and he wouldn't stay upright in the unnecessary pillow/rest thing we'd bought him. It was getting a bit fraught so I sat in the back with him. Mum and Jayne were waiting for us at our house and it was so lovely to see them.

'Hello Chilton family,' Mum said beaming. She was standing in the door with my apron on and I could smell roast lamb cooking. I'm home, I thought. Please God let my thoughts and feelings relax now and my mind be at peace.

'Glass of wine 'Mummy'?' said Jayne. But I couldn't take in what they were saying. I was aware I was smiling, but whilst life was going on as normal around me, my world was in slow motion. I was made to sit down whilst Chris got me a drink and handed me a little bag. In it was a fridge magnet, which read 'World's Best Mummy'. So, let's recap here, I'd spent the last few days in the depths of birthing hell, had my stomach cut open after a very long labour, received a blood transfusion and had about two hours' sleep in three days and all I got was a fucking fridge magnet. We have integrated units so have nowhere to stick it, although I can think of somewhere right now and if I had the energy I'd do it. I didn't even say thank you.

We sat down to lunch and Mum proposed a toast, 'To Sarah, Chris and Johnathan. God bless you all and I hope you all have a long, happy and healthy life together.' We all chinked glasses and I started crying. I just couldn't stop. The lunch looked gorgeous but I was too tired to even eat anything. Mum insisted I got some sleep and said that if Johnathan woke for a feed then she'd come and get me. I was just so sorry that they'd spent time and money on my coming home lunch but all I wanted to do was sleep and forget everything. I remember Jayne shooting concerned looks at Mum. Chris was tucking into his lunch by this time, oblivious to everything.

I went upstairs and collapsed on the bed. I'd been asleep no longer than fifteen minutes when Jayne was waking me up saying that Johnathan was crying. She went and got him for me. I couldn't think straight and just waited for Jayne to bring him up for a feed. I sat in the nursery, the room I'd sat in days before feeling excitement, nerves, slight trepidation about what lay ahead but mainly feeling impatient as I just wanted the baby out so that I could get on with being a Mum and doing what all other new parents do – get back on with life. I could never have envisaged that, five days later, I would be feeling shock, exhaustion, disappointment, regret, sadness and panic.

Jayne brought Johnathan into me and I did the very best I could at putting him into the best breast-feeding position. I felt so clumsy, Jayne tried her best to help me but between us we were making things worse and Johnathan was getting agitated. Please, just let me sleep I thought. I started to cry again and called for Chris. He told me not to worry and said I'd be fine. He wants me to give breastfeeding a go and persevere and see what happen after a few days. A few days? He may as well have said a few years. It's hurting more than words could say and feels weird. Johnathan's still not latching on properly and his tongue is still 'clicking' and is subsequently getting annoyed because he's obviously so hungry and I just want to bolt myself in the bedroom and sleep 'til Christmas. I need time to evaluate what I've been through.

I eventually managed to satisfy Johnathan and Mum put him back to sleep in the moses basket where he slept for three hours before waking me up for another feed. By this time Mum and Jayne had gone and it was just Chris and I. We got into bed together and cuddled up. The look he gave me was strange; perhaps he's worried about me. He gave me a big hug, a hug he's never given me before, again, probably worried about me. I promptly fell asleep to be woken up two hours later by Johnathan crying and me covered in sweat and shivering with the cold. Welcome to motherhood Sarah. It's certainly not doing what it says on the tin.

Chapter 4

Being a Mum

Raising kids is part joy and part guerrilla warfare.
Ed Asner

Intolerant Tuesday, June.

Michelle and her daughter Sienna came to see Johnathan today. Michelle is lovely but she talks for Britain. I wanted to shout 'Shut the fuck up Michelle!' Sienna was filling me in on every bloody thing Johnathan did. I know she's only eleven and was in her element holding him but if she told me once she told me fifty times that he'd yawned, slightly moved his right arm, twitched, pooped, opened his eyes, closed them again. It didn't seem right to get up and scream 'Get out, for fuck's sake!' so I had to grin and bear them for an hour. I cannot begin to tell you how much I resented them for leaving me to do whatever they wanted. They waved goodbye at the door and were going to walk into town to watch a film. Why didn't they offer to take Johnathan off me for a bit? Couldn't they see I was shattered?

Friday

I have no one to confide in. Chris thinks I'll be fine, Mum thinks I'm just tired and Jayne is too far away. I saw a friend today and when I told her I had stupid thoughts about leaving Johnathan out in the drive on a rainy day, or leaving him in the house crying, she just laughed at me. My health visitor thinks I'm okay and if I say I'm not, she'll be annoyed because 'this' is what I 'wanted', so I guess I just need to get on with it. So, it looks like it's just me and you darling Diary. I feel really stupid. My ideas about being a Mum have been completely unrealistic. In those bloody magazines I read, I saw photographs of mothers with 'their' babies, looking happy, contented, slim, and not a single bag under their eyes! I bet it had taken hours to get that one shot of the baby smiling and the woman was just a model, who had slept incredibly well the night before. Bitch.

I read magazines about childbirth, watched baby programmes, which, in my opinion, having been through the realities of childbirth, should be banned. It didn't prepare me for the birth because I was convinced everything was going to go smoothly, just like the births I'd seen on the television. (They're hardly likely to show us the ones that don't go to plan are they, with mothers who are terrified, miserable and suffering from shock and lack of sleep, like me?)

What makes me sad the most is the depiction of mothers having that wonderful 'skin-to-skin' experience. I was out for the count when Johnathan was born and wouldn't have known if they'd placed a herd of elephants on me. I never cuddled him and that makes me sad. These programmes then show us the family at home a couple of weeks later and everyone looking happy and well rested. They should have filmed mine; and interviewed me at home two weeks later. I'd give them some home truths about motherhood, which would reduce the birth rate worldwide. My house looks like it's been raided by the police in search of drugs and I still look like I could have won an audition for a horror movie. If I don't improve, come Halloween people will congratulate me on my 'terrifying' outfit and make-up.

Another thing – adverts for baby products or washing powder, what a con. Happy babies who play and go to sleep without a problem because they've been bathed in some magic lotion. Utter bollocks. I really did think I'd prepared myself to be a Mum. And where the hell has my independence gone? On maternity leave, I was still able to 'pop out'. I'm really resenting not being able to do what I want without having to lug a baby bag the size of Europe everywhere with me and the worries of, 'Will he wake up?' 'Is he hungry?' 'Is he hot, is he cold?' 'Does his nappy need changing?' 'Has he got wind?' 'What happens if he's sick in the pram and I'm in the middle of town?' Oh God, I hope I feel better soon.

Fuckin' Thursday

Johnathan is two weeks old today and Chris is going away tomorrow night on a TA mission. I can't believe he's leaving me on my own. Apparently it's one of those compulsory weekends. I have no idea how I'll cope. At least he is going to be back in time for the two of us to go to the evening wedding party of my friend, Max, on the Saturday night – I'm really looking forward to a night out, getting all dressed up and feeling like me again. Mum's going to baby sit for us, bless her.

Tits Up Tuesday

What a horrible few days I've had. Chris left on the Friday morning at 8.00ish and I knew then that I was on my own until late Saturday afternoon. I managed a quick shower and washed my hair whilst Johnathan was sleeping but I never got around to drying it. Johnathan started crying as soon as I got out and I didn't even get dressed because when I put him down he cried. I was tired beyond belief and he was probably picking up on my anxious mood. A lot of the day was a haze to be honest, all I can remember is curling up on the sofa with him, trying to persevere with breast feeding and failing dismally. He was getting upset and I just kept crying and felt so tense. When Chris got home on the Saturday afternoon, I'd not even dressed from the day before or dried my hair. It looked very wild. Johnathan and I were still curled up on the sofa and Chris could see the look of despair on my face. I just desperately wanted to sleep and for this baby to go away. There was no way I could face going to Max's evening reception because I know I would have just spent the whole night crying. My eyes looked like I'd had a bad reaction to something, they were so puffy. Chris took Johnathan over to

Mum's for me, put in a brief appearance at the evening do and sent my apologies. I was finally on my own. I needed this space to take stock of things. Since being a Mum I hadn't had any time whatsoever to do this. I had hit the ground and crashed, badly, my brain couldn't cope with being endlessly pounded with new things to process and learn.

I ran a bath, a really deep one with bubble bath in it and poured myself a glass of much needed red wine. I had no thought about the affect of breast feeding Johnathan and drinking wine. Truth be told, I didn't care. I sat in the bath and cried until I had run out of tears. I can only describe my thoughts as utter disappointment. I had grown this baby inside me for nine months and had looked forward to welcoming him into the world so very much. Friends, midwives, even strangers, kept saying things like, 'Oh how exciting, I bet you can't wait for baby to arrive', 'Oh it's such a wonderful experience, you'll be fine.' What have I done wrong? No matter how much I rack my brain I can't think where I've gone wrong.

When I got out of the bath I wrapped myself in a towel, sat on the loo and sobbed my heart out, again. 'Please help me, please help me, I don't know what to do, I really don't know what to do.' I felt an overwhelming wave of panic suddenly hit me because I know I've made a real whopper of a mistake in having a baby and there's nothing I can do about it. I can't write it off as 'one of those things' and learn not to do it again. It's not a bad purchase where I can go back for a refund. I then snuggled up inside my dressing gown, curled up on the sofa with another glass of red wine and watched television. For a split second, it was like life had reverted back to how it was before I got pregnant. It was lovely, as if a bad dream had ended and life was back to normal. It may have been a split second, but it seemed to last for a long time. I felt so happy in that time and worry free.

But my next thought was Oh shit, he's got to bring the baby back home soon. I fell asleep on the sofa and woke up to blue flashing lights outside the house. Apparently, a car had been stolen and abandoned outside Barbara and Neil's. At that point, Chris arrived home with Johnathan in his car seat, just as the police woman was outside our house. I felt an overwhelming sense of protectiveness towards Johnathan and just wanted him inside with me. Whilst this made me feel better about my thoughts, I know there is still something not right with me.

Thursday, July.
Think I've developed Tourette's syndrome. Plus, very rarely in my life have I ever wanted to inflict physical harm to so many people. I cannot bloody help it if my baby decides to wake up in the supermarket and scream blue sodding murder. I'm sorry everyone for not knowing where the fucking off switch is. If I did, do you think I'd put up with screaming so high pitched that all dogs in the surrounding area react to it? No, I bloody wouldn't so cut me some slack for God's sake. It took me all morning to get out of the house because Johnathan decided to puke up his milk and then promptly shit some of it out just as I was leaving. I haven't slept well and Chris is away for two weeks with the fucking TA. Do not, I repeat, do not mess with 'The Mummy' today, as she cannot be held responsible for her actions. I actually feel like I could do an SAS sleep deprivation course and beat even the most experienced soldier. And breathe Sarah.

Sorry Di, I do feel slightly better for that, but am concerned that I don't really want to do anything or to even see anyone. If I do go and see my doctor it will mean owning up to the fact that I'm not coping or happy, which may then lead to having to talk to someone and I can't be arsed to speak to myself in the mirror anymore so I really don't think I'll want to speak to some condescending health visitor who will no doubt give me concerned looks and give my worries lip service. I'll be put on a six-month waiting list for counselling and what's the use in that? I need help now. How can I admit that I'm not happy being a Mum?

They may take Johnathan away from me and what the hell would that do to Chris? Everyone thinks I'm happy but when I'm on my own I'm crying a lot. It can't be baby blues still can it? I'm still getting these stupid 'what if' thoughts. Yesterday I worried about if I left Johnathan in his car seat all day in the car and forgot about him, and left him in there overnight. How the hell can I say that to my doctor? Before you know it, I'll be in a straight jacket, sitting in a padded cell and dribbling. Don't know why I'd be dribbling but I just imagine people in straight jackets dribbling. I think I'm just going to have to get on with this and figure out a way to recover on my own.

Sodding Sunday

Mum came over today and did the night feeds for me whilst Chris is still away. She's reassured me not to feel bad about not breastfeeding. I've given it six weeks and my nipples are now slowly beginning to grow back and actually look their normal colour, as opposed to blood red, green with infection, bits missing, hard and lumpy. Really sexy, no wonder there's nothing happening between the sheets at the moment with Chris and I. Mum's also passed on her wisdom of getting Johnathan into a routine. Apparently, four hourly feeds are the way she got me sleeping through the night and to be a contended baby. So, from hereon in Johnathan will be fed at ten, two, six and ten (ish).

I miss Chris terribly. He's phoned once since he's been away but said that the signal's not very good in the base he's stationed at. He's due back in three days, on his birthday actually, so I'm going to make him his favourite coffee and walnut cake whilst Johnathan has his lunch time nap. I've made a Welcome Home Daddy sign with a photo of Johnathan on the bottom too. It looks so cute. Chris told me not to wait up for him when he comes back as he'll be late. I put the sign on the door and went to bed. My cold has really taken hold now and I feel awful and lifeless. Chris came in at 11.00pm and came upstairs. I managed to say, 'Hello, how are you? Happy Birthday.'

'Hi, I'm fine, sorry you're not well, get some sleep, I'll sleep in the spare room'. With that he kissed my forehead and went to bed. Johnathan woke up at 6.30am and I sat on the edge of my bed getting accustomed to the pounding in my head. Chris was dead to the world so I left him and gave Johnathan his milk. It had gone 10.00am before Chris awoke. I went in, giving him his cards, presents and coffee and walnut cake.

'Are you okay? You seem very quiet'.

'Yeah fine, just tired. It was a good two weeks to be honest, but lots to think about. You look terrible, why don't you get back to bed and I'll sort out my washing and look after Johnathan'.

'But Chris it's your birthday I'm so sorry'.

'Don't be silly, you need to rest, I'm sure it's been hectic for you the last two weeks'.

I slept for five hours, my body so grateful for the chance to switch off for a while. A couple of days later, I'm still noticing that Chris is quiet and pensive.

'Are you sure you're okay, you've been very quiet since you came back'.

'Have I? Sorry, yes I'm fine, honestly'.

'Sure? I want to make sure you're happy too. Having a baby isn't all about me and I want you to tell me if something's bothering you.'

'Honestly Sarah, hand on heart, I'm happy and nothing's wrong'. With that he kissed my forehead and put the kettle on. I feel happier now having heard that, but I'm wondering if something happened whilst he was away that he didn't want to tell me. I've spoken to friends and nothing untoward apparently happened. I'm sure it's nothing, just Post Natal Paranoia probably.

Friday, September.
Evening Di. Apologies, it's been three months since I made an

entry into what is turning out to be the diary of a crap, disillusioned, knackered, Mum. Latest news is as follows, and is in no particular order...

1. Nipples fully restored to former glory.
2. Still feel knackered, more mentally, but Johnathan sleeping through the night thanks to Mum's four hourly feed tip.
3. Chris and I have had sex. Not brilliant and I initiated it, but it was still sex.
4. Went to a baby group recently and actually laughed – at the women, not with them, unfortunately. I really don't want to sit and have a conversation with a woman who thinks it's absolutely fine to flop out her 38GG and attach baby to it. Has she not heard of the word 'discretion'?

Another thing, I couldn't give a fuck if the wheels on the bus go round and round. I know they do, how else would it move, so I don't need to sing a song about it. I'd like to sing my own song, 'The Mummies on the bus shout I want a glass of wine and a nice long sleep, a nice long sleep'. This group is actually a fashion parade, not necessarily for the Mums but their babies. Why? It's not going to enhance their childhood by being in the latest trendy clothes. Sorry, one more thing, someone needs to tell these women that parenthood is not a competition. Does it really matter if your baby is sitting up before someone else's? No. Does it matter that you've weaned little Johnny at fourteen weeks when no one else has? No. I swear if someone else sprouts unnecessary bilge like that again, I'm going to announce that, at fifteen weeks, Johnathan can count to ten, use a knife and fork, read his own bedtime stories and is potty trained.

So, on a scale of 1-10, I guess I feel 6. I know I'm not perfect but I'm getting there slowly. I'm realising now that the whole birth thing was a shock and the reality is miles different to the expectation. I've also got to realise that some women maybe feeling like me too, but putting on a façade in company. I saw a woman in town the other day, pushing her pram, baby similar age to Johnathan. She looked slim, pretty, happy and content. I looked and thought 'why cant I feel and look like her?' Mind you, who's to say she wasn't thinking the same about me? Things aren't always as they seem are they?

Chapter 5

Losing a Husband

If someone you love hurts you cry a river, build a bridge, and get over it.
Anon

Wednesday
Not happy. Chris away with work again, won't be back until Sunday afternoon. We've not spent much time together lately. Johnathan has the cold from hell and Chris slept through it all – even when I screamed at Johnathan to shut up. Felt guilty afterwards, not his fault, but bloody hell it felt good to release the tension. Anyway, I'm knackered and now have four nights to cope with it all on my own. Oh, I wonder what joys await me...

I had the delights of 'Tearaway Tiddlers' this morning. When will these Mums realise that I'm not like them? Jo-Jo's on the floor propped up by some germ ridden, salmonella coated, baby toy, on his own, for a reason. I need coffee, toast, earplugs and a sleep please. Jo-Jo's cough and cold is keeping me awake at night so why would I want to interact with him when there are other babies here for him to engage with? My life does not, and will not, revolve around him. I desperately need some time to myself. It's almost like I've got a backlog of paperwork to go through, of thoughts, feelings, emotions etc, from when he was born. It's mounting up on a daily basis and getting me down because I haven't processed it and soon I'll scream, chuck it all up in the air and shout endless expletives. I'm really not coping with this at all and the tiredness is just killing me.

Gee, I can't wait for the next instalment. Will Sarah get a good night's sleep? Will Jo-Jo cough all night long again? What will Sarah have for breakfast? Will she be able to sit down in peace and eat it? How many bottles will she sterilise in one day? Will Jo-Jo be sick again? Tune in next time folks for the next exciting instalment of *Life in the Fast Lane* by Sarah 'Shit Mum' Chilton.

Friday
Had a manicure today, followed by a full body massage from Troy, 6ft Australian, tanned and toned body. Went for lunch with the girls, had too much wine, got tipsy, got a taxi home, curled up in front of the television with a cuppa, huge bar of chocolate and watched a black and white movie. Then I woke up. I can dream can't I? In reality, I had about five hours broken sleep. Johnathan coughing again, went shopping, came home, unpacked it whilst Johnathan napped. Chris phoned and annoyed me because he sounded very happy, relaxed, and was about to go down for dinner. When I reminded him what I was going through he didn't seem interested. When he comes home on Sunday, I shall hand Johnathan to him and go for a well-earned sleep. I'm actually looking forward to going back to work next week, where there will be proper fully grown adults and no talk of babies. Sheer bliss.

Sunday bloody Sunday (worst day of my life thus far)
I don't know where to begin. If I thought life was stressful forty eight hours ago, it's certainly taken one massive whopper of a turn for the worse now. I had a feeling something wasn't right when Chris phoned me to say that the course on the Saturday had finished but he would be home on Sunday as there was a disco on the Saturday night that he wanted to go to. 'What? You want to go to a disco instead of coming home to help me and see your son?' 'Yes, it's been a long week and I want to relax with my work colleagues'. Now, this was said in a really defiant and adamant way. I felt a wave of hot panic ensue me and I realised that something wasn't right.

Chris arrived just after lunch on Sunday. It was so nice to hear his car reversing into the drive because it meant that I had someone to mentally release some of the pressure from me and I needed a big hug and reassurance from him. I'd missed him and didn't like being on my own. He stepped into the house and just calmly said, 'We need to talk. There's someone else and I'm leaving you.'

It makes me sick to write those words. I was devastated and sick to the core that these words left the mouth of my husband, the man I loved beyond words. I was holding Johnathan and nearly dropped him with shock. I don't know how Chris managed to be so nonchalant about it all. My whole world imploded in a split second and I have no idea what to do. My thoughts went wild, with who, what, why, where, when? I asked if it was someone I knew but he just laughed at me and said no. Strange, I never found that question funny at all. What a bastard. It transpires that it's someone who works for his firm, but she's from a branch up north, Mary. That explained the trips up north to help out the new branch; however, Chris's idea of helping went beyond the call of duty. Half an hour earlier she was just a person. A person who's wrecked my life and home. Now 'it' has a name. Chris didn't find it funny when I said that a biblical name is hardly fitting for a 'Slapper' who sleeps with married men and denies a five month old baby the presence of his father for the rest of his life.

As soon as Chris told me, it was like he had been released. He took off his wedding ring and started whistling around the house. He went and sat on the wall outside in the back garden. I asked him what we'd do with the house and he said, whilst surveying it in a way I took to be his ticket out of here, 'We'll sell the house, there's a lot of equity in it now, split the proceeds and go our separate ways.' I then realised why he insisted on going ahead with the extension. He wasn't thinking of my welfare at all then was he? The weeks I spent freezing cold in the middle of winter because the heating was off, doors open all day and no cooker so it was either a ping meal or takeaway. The house was like a building site but never once did he try and make it easier, and safer, for me to get around.

I couldn't take it all in. Go our separate ways? Who has Johnathan then? Me? He'd obviously chatted this over with 'Slapper Features' and got it all sussed out. I doubt he'd even been on a course this weekend and I felt stupid for believing him. I threw my wedding rings at him and phoned Mum and was strangely calm, 'Well, you'll never guess what Mum; Chris is leaving me for another woman'. I said it in a way you'd tell someone Sainsbury's aren't doing their 3-for-2 on wine when the offer was supposed to last another week. She was lost for words and I wish I'd just driven over to see her rather than ring up and blurt it out the way I did. I'll never understand how I didn't crash the car on the way to Mum's as I don't remember the journey at all.

She was in shock when I got there. I just broke down crying and couldn't stop. Mum phoned Jayne, and we had a three way conversation. I couldn't take it all in as it was something else for me to process and I already felt like my head would explode with excess 'paperwork'. I then phoned my boss Andy. He was also lost for words and was more than happy to give me a couple of weeks off. I'm due to start back to work next week, so I feel really guilty now. My whole world has fallen apart. I didn't want to go back home after being with Mum. Two of Chris's TA friends were in the garden with Chris when I got back and they stayed with him for hours. They sheepishly said bye to me when they left and I was left in the house with a man who'd just torn my world apart without a second thought. How can someone you've spent several years with just switch off their emotions? When I said to him that I needed to be on my own, the look of disgust on his face at having to stay in the same bedroom as me was sickening and so very hurtful. Seven days beforehand, life was relatively normal. I can't take all of this in. He's not speaking to me now and can't even bear to look at me. I don't know what I've done wrong. What the hell am I going to do? Where's my Chris gone? I don't think I can do this anymore. How the hell am I going to cope with Johnathan on my own?

Monday

Andy got me an appointment with one of his solicitor contacts and I went today. One of Mum's friends, Gina, went with me as my head was mush from practically no sleep the night before and having just realised that my husband had been having an affair through the conception, pregnancy and birth of our son. I couldn't retain anything. Mum stayed at mine and looked after Johnathan. Straightaway, I was advised that Chris is not entitled to half of the house, which, I have to say, actually put a smile on my face. I'm annoyed that 'Slapper Features' won't be named in the proceedings; I wanted her named and shamed. Why did we banish the stocks?

Tuesday

I think I'm actually going slightly mad. It's only been a few days since Chris, who, from now on, will be called 'Twat Face' or 'TF' announced his 'news'. I have started to get a bit angry with him because when he gets up for work in the morning, it's as if Johnathan doesn't exist. I expected to disappear from Chris's radar, but not Johnathan, not his son, his only child. I asked if he could give him his milk this morning, to which he replied, 'No, I've got to get to work.' It's the callous wiping hands of every parenting responsibility that has truly shocked and hurt me. I need to grow some balls and learn to stick up for myself. I'm realising that Chris is actually the selfish one, not me, and I think he's used me over the years and made sure that he's okay.

Wednesday

Evening Di, angry Sarah is coming out now. Twat Face said

something really horrible to me today. I plucked up courage to speak to him and have to say that I'm finding him repulsive. I hate him. I feel such a prat for wasting my time on this man who obviously gets bored of relationships every few years and finds it easy to discard them for a new 'toy'. (Perhaps his first wife wasn't the one who had the initial affair?) Anyway, I asked him why he'd done this to me. I know that I'd never treat him like this. He replied that there were things about me he just couldn't change or won't change. What an absolute load of bollocking crap. What sort of a reason is that? I know that one day I'll laugh about all of this. There are things about everyone you 'can't change or won't change', but you don't treat them like something nasty on the bottom of your shoe. I didn't say this to him, because I couldn't be arsed wasting my breath but I thought of all the things about him that I'd like to change i.e. blowing his nose in the shower, spending too much money, leaving his work crap everywhere in the house, making it obvious to all and sundry that he's just had a crap because a: it stinks and b: I can still see part of it down the pan. The list is quite lengthy but I can't be arsed to carry on, excuse the pun.

Thursday

Tackling my financial plight is next on my agenda. I was dreading this day, and as I feared it has been mentally exhausting. Jo-Jo was at nursery so I went to Mum's and phoned the Council, CSA, Child Tax Office and Benefits Office. I got cross with myself because I cried when one woman decided it was perfectly acceptable to talk down to me. Mind you, she started being nicer when I told her that three weeks ago life was plodding on normally, I didn't ask my husband to leave me and have an affair whilst I was pregnant, so I was terribly sorry if she obviously didn't want to talk to me judging by the attitude she was giving me, but I needed her to do her job, and needed her help. It was horrible.

The day did end pretty well for me though. When I got back from Mum's, Twat Face was cooking his dinner on the five-burner hob (he'd insisted on having) and whistling away as if he didn't have a care in the world. I plucked up courage and asked him when he'd be moving out. I can't bear being in the same room as him now but we need to discuss things and this is just torture.

'I don't know when I'm going,' he replied in a na na, na, na na way. It was like a five year old quite frankly. Then something inside me just snapped. This overwhelming rage surged up and I knew that I had to physically hurt him. It was no good punching him as a: he had his back to me and where would I punch him? and b: I couldn't punch my way out of a paper bag and it would have had no effect on him and he would have laughed at me. So, with my slip on leather mules I quite calmly walked over to him and kicked him on his calf with all the strength I had. Oh my god it felt better than an orgasm (and it was spontaneous unlike the spontaneous sex I always tried Chris to try).

'Ouch, that hurt,' he said looking really rather shocked and exasperated.

'Good, I hope it fucking hurt.' I retorted and stormed out. I drove to Michelle's house in a right state because I just can't stand being in the same house as him for much longer. It's like he's mentally bullying me. He needs to leave very soon.

Monday, October.
TF thankfully moved out on Friday. He's not limping as much as he was after the kick I gave him. My slip on leather mules made quite a dent in his calf! It was the weirdest day. I took Jo-Jo to nursery and decided to buy myself something nice for dinner. I bought some homemade burgers, lovely salad bits and a bottle of red wine. I wanted to be at home just in case TF decided to take things he shouldn't. Funnily enough I didn't trust him. He'd hired

a van and made several trips back and forth. I felt like a prisoner in my own home that day. He spent a lot of time on the phone too obviously talking to 'her'. I went to pick Jo-Jo up from nursery at 5.00pm and I was so hoping TF would have gone by the time I got back, but it was dark and nearly 7.00pm when he finally left. The house was freezing because he kept the door open all day. One bit of crap he was taking was a little parting gift from me. I'd won a plastic rose, set in gel to look like water, in a glass vase, in some stupid raffle. I'd never gotten around to putting it in a charity bag so decided to give it to TF. I wrapped a little message around it and buried it in his box to be opened with Slapper Features when moving into their perfect house to live their perfect life. The note read, 'This rose represents our marriage – fake.'

As TF left he just said he would be in touch to get the rest of his stuff. He said good-bye to Jo-Jo and that was it. If he could have erased me out of his life then I think he would have done. After all we'd been through, all I had was 'I'll be in touch about the rest of my stuff'. The whole situation is very sad and I felt numb when he went. I put Jo-Jo to bed who, thankfully, was oblivious to the whole thing. My stomach was churning but I was determined to relax with my lovely dinner and enjoy a glass of wine. The house was so quiet, like it was trying to be considerate towards to me but deep down not knowing what to do or say. It also felt like the aftermath of a tornado. You can see it coming, it hits you and consumes you and once it's gone you're left to deal with the carnage it leaves. I feel so very sad, alone and frightened about what the future is going to bring me. What the hell am I going to do? I've never lived on my own before, let alone looked after a baby, whose life I've not come to terms with yet. I spent most Friday night in the bathroom being sick. Motherhood? I sure as hell never signed up for *this*.

Why me? Wednesday, November.

I need to buy a red light bulb for my outside light. I had to laugh today, because if I didn't I would have cried and not stopped. I've got to pay for the privilege of divorcing my adulterous husband. I've got legal aid but my monthly repayments are just ridiculous. On top of that I've got to pay nursery fees and the mortgage, totalling just under £1000 per month. It may as well be £3000. I think I also need to leave some calling cards in phone boxes.

Monday (losing the will to live)

I get through the day knowing that I can have some peace and sleep at the end of it. My head is constantly filled with sterilising, liquidising, washing, ironing, tidying away, and scraping bits of baby food (or sick, who knows what) off me. So at the end of yet another day being me, the Mum who sometimes can't cope, I sit down with my friend, Cabernet Shiraz. He's great, really relaxes me and I forget all my worries; money, bills, work, car, shopping, Jo-Jo to name but a few... I have many other friends like Rioja, Chardonnay and Rosé. They don't talk much but have this natural ability to let me 'chill'. Especially on Saturday nights. I hate weekends; they remind me I'm on my own. Friends at work talk about what their plans are at the weekend. Oh how I envy these people. I work part time and have Mondays off. For the first time in my working life I dread the weekends. Three days of depressing boredom lying ahead of me. I get up at 6.30am, even at weekends, so that I'm ready for when Jo-Jo wakes up because I can't even have a shower now without him trying to join me and it's just too stressful to attempt it. When I go in and get him up an hour later I just think of the next twelve hours ahead of me before it's his bed time. I think back to the old days of partying, going to see friends, having friends over and getting drunk. Granted, I can still get drunk, and quite often do, but that's it. My life is dull.

Anyway, this Saturday I had an early night. At 2.00am I woke up to hear Jo-Jo coughing. Two coughs and a nasty, squelchy burp sound, followed by a really distressed cry. Isn't it amazing how you can just get up and put yourself into action even though you've quaffed too much wine and are in the middle of having a gorgeous dream about a sexy man? I shook myself to life and rushed into Jo-Jo's room.

It was covered in sick. I wanted to cordon off the area and call the crime squad. How the hell could something so small produce so much vomit? He was in his cot, which, typically, had fresh bedding on. I'm so glad I went for the cream colour when choosing my perfectly kitted out nursery. It was now every colour of the rainbow and smelt like a cesspit. The beautiful cream carpet was also covered in it. I think the only bit of the room that Jo-Jo excluded from his projectile vomit display was the outside window sill. Where the hell do I start? I got Jo-Jo out of his cot and took his grow bag off and his jimjams. The room smelt so bad I had to fight back my own 'contribution'.

Now came the bit where I shouted at TF in my head. How on earth do I cope with this? Jo-Jo was shivering with shock and cold because he was naked and wet and I'd stepped in a mixture of cottage pie and yogurt. I had to put Jo-Jo down, take off my jimjams, wipe my feet with them, rush to the airing cupboard, cover Jo-Jo in a towel, scoop practically everything in his room into a towel which left some tumble weed floating across, carry him in one arm to the kitchen, and the contents of his bedroom in the wrapped up towel in the other. I'd forgotten I was naked from the waist down, put the kitchen light on and cursed myself for being too tipsy to pull the blinds across. Everything got bundled into the washing machine and put on the 'severe and stinky baby sick' cycle. When I'd 'de-sicked' Jo-Jo and sat him down in his new bedding gear, he looked up at me in a really sad and pathetic way, poor thing. I sat propped up against pillows with him next to me surrounded by a sea of towels.

It was 6.45am when I awoke with a shooting pain in my neck having slept bolt upright and I was so, so tired. I cried at the thought of having to practically gut Jo-Jo's room, scrub the carpet, and bleach his bedding and wash the mattress, whilst looking after him – I didn't sign up to be a single Mum! Chris committed us both to starting a family when he was having an affair and planning a cosy little life with Slapper Features. He's not even given me a second thought. I'm so exhausted, and I hate this life.

Tuesday

For once in my life, words escape me. Twat Face and I have been exchanging various emails and I've had to print out the following as it has to be seen to be believed.

Chris, I don't seem to have received a reply to my recent email. As mentioned, I have ordered a new wardrobe and wish to put this in the fourth bedroom. Please would you arrange for all your boxes to be collected next week, otherwise I shall dispose of them myself. Thank you.

Sarah, I did respond, which is a shame as you seem to have ordered the replacement wardrobe. If you haven't ordered the wardrobe, do you want to buy the other one back? The place I am going to would seem to have wardrobes fitted. Let me know. The boxes are being moved by the end of next weekend. I have paid my Mess bill at £98.60, which includes the Summer Ball we went to in August. Can you let me know how you wish to clear your half?

Chris, thanks for the offer of the wardrobe, but I've got one on order now. Asking me if I wanted to buy my own wardrobe back did make me, and everyone who read the email, laugh. However, Johnathan is fine and getting over his cough not that you're aware he had one as you've not been in touch since you left. As I work on a Tues/Wed/Fri and don't get home until at least 5.45pm it would probably be better if you came to see him on a Mon/Thurs at 5.00pm. That way you could feed, bath and put him to bed. I think it would be best for us to arrange permanent visits.

As regards the Ball tickets, again, this made me laugh! We attended your function as a couple and therefore, I have no intention of paying you for something I attended as your wife. However, any disputes I suggest we put through our Solicitors. I cannot afford much at the moment as I need to buy Johnathan some winter jumpers. You've made so many people laugh with your email Chris, do keep them coming!

What a prat. When I think back to that Ball it was a complete disaster from start to finish. Mum had Jo-Jo overnight for us and I was so looking forward to dressing up and having a night out in a posh hotel. Chris got drunk and spent most of the evening with his friends and left me to talk babies with the other women. I wanted a night off from all that shite, thanks very much. The next morning, I drove back to Mum's because Chris was so hung over from the previous night and kept chucking up on various gutters on the way back... Needless to say he was no good to man or beast for the rest of the day so I was left to look after Jo-Jo.

Wednesday

Phoned my bank. TF hasn't set up the standing order for the agreed £50 per week. He paid me £50 cash last Monday and said he'd set up the standing order. He also didn't pay in his salary, which he promised me he would do, as the bombshell he threw at me would have left me short. 'Of course I'll pay my salary in, don't panic' was his sarcastic reply when I asked him for reassurance. So, when I asked him why, he just said they had expenses too. (I really do need to sort out that red light bulb.) I have two choices. I either let this beat me to the ground, let my mood do its worst and make Jo-Jo's childhood be a sad one; or, I dust myself off, accept that I cannot change what's happened and find a way to get better and look ahead to the future. I'm going to choose the latter, I'm not going to let that bastard grind me down. In such a short space of time I'm learning so much about myself. I didn't know I was so strong. I even killed my first spider yesterday! I was in the unnecessarily built study and it ran across the hall. It was so big I heard it mutter 'shit she's seen me' as it ran by. I just ran across and jumped on it and felt very proud of myself. It was such a small thing to do, but such a big step for me. I'm coming to terms with being a Mum a lot more now. I'm still in my routine, which has helped no end. Jo-Jo is fed at four hourly intervals 6am 10am 2pm and 6pm, plus a sleep feed at 10.00pm. I know I'll have my down days but that's life and I'll get through it. I'm finding depression depressing so need to get on with life.

Thursday

Twat Face came tonight at 5.00pm. He said he'd sent an email but our system is playing up at work. It was very sad to see, but he doesn't know how to interact with Jo-Jo. The last time he saw him was the day he moved out, which was October. Previous to that, he hasn't spent any quality time with him. Jo-Jo was extremely upset and couldn't stop crying. I picked him up and he was fine. He doesn't know Twat Face and is picking up on the fact that he's unsure around him. If he's only going to see him in an evening he'll never know him properly enough for me to be confident to take him away for a night. Jo-Jo certainly won't know Slapper Features and she doesn't have children. What an arse.

Monday

Morning Di, get this. I received a letter from Richards Estate Agents addressed to Twat Face and Slapper Features today. I was shaking with rage and extremely upset. I opened the letter because I wanted to know why on earth I would receive a letter for them to my home. I phoned TF and asked him why and he told me to wind my neck in, he had no idea. Wind my neck in? I've never wished halitosis, alopecia and impotence on one man, all at the same time, with such conviction. I think what hurts me the most is his lack of compassion. I'm trying to rebuild my life and I get mail for *them* at my home, confirming *their* new address and tenancy agreement for *their* new life together. What does he want me to do? Buy them a present? Stupid man. He's being so nasty and vindictive towards me and it really hurts. If I hadn't received this letter today I would never have known for sure where he was moving to. I asked him the other day how he would manage to see Jo-Jo if he moved out of the area. He bit my head off and barked, 'I'll be here and our son's name is Johnathan not Jo-Jo'. If he wasn't going to tell me where he was, how does he expect me to be confident at him taking Jo-Jo for the night at some time in the future? I've started saying Jo-Jo as I think it suits him and I like it, but now that I know TF hates it I'll say it even more! He is such an arse.

TF came by later on and apologised for being a twat earlier (no Di, he didn't use those exact words!) Mum was here and we made him feel very welcome. Mum made him a cup of tea (resisting the temptation to drop a couple of laxatives in as we'd laughed about earlier). Jo-Jo was a very happy boy anyway, but TF isn't relaxed with him. It was very silent in the kitchen when he was giving Jo-Jo his milk. Does he really want anything to do with him?

Thursday
TF came tonight and everything was going well. I offered him a drink and he'd bought a couple of things for Jo-Jo to play with in the bath. I'm trying really hard to make things easy but he just starts with the sarcastic attitude. I shut myself away in the lounge and cried. I can't go through this every time he comes. All I ever did was love him and he's treating me like I was the one who had the affair. I want to encourage TF to see more of Jo-Jo because I never had a relationship with my Dad when he left and I don't want that for Jo-Jo. I need to make a doll and buy some really sharp pins!

Monday

It was my wedding anniversary this weekend. I went to see TF's step Dad, Derek and the family in Bristol. It was weird being in the house TF grew up in, with just Derek. He's never recovered from the death of TF's Mum, Vera, a couple of years ago. It was all very sudden and even though she hadn't enjoyed the best of health for a long time, her death was very tragic. TF respected her a lot and valued her opinion on various things. When his Dad, Roy, walked out years ago, after having an affair (like father like son) he was there for Vera and helped her get over it. I personally think he went off the rails a bit when she died, as he had no one to answer to really did he? He couldn't have had an affair during her lifetime, not after the way he slated Roy for what he did to Vera. Anyway, I digress. The day was taken up seeing all TF's family, Vera's Sisters, his cousins and some aunts, who have been so supportive towards me. Derek wasn't great and didn't help me with Jo-Jo at all. I'd had a two hour journey and he just sat in the lounge whilst I got everything in from the car so I didn't feel very welcome from the off. He made dinner when everyone had gone and I felt so drained from putting on an act for everyone. I just wanted to scream and drive back home. No one really wanted to talk about what Chris had done and I did. They are such lovely people and I don't think they knew what to say. All this paperwork from when Jo-Jo was born is still piling up and needs processing and filing. I phoned Mum on Sunday morning and said that I wasn't going to stay for lunch with Derek and that I just wanted to go. Derek didn't really seem happy with this, but quite frankly I couldn't have cared less what anyone thought, I just needed to breathe and get out of that house. It was too soon for me to have gone up, but Derek asked me and I thought it would be nice. Mum was at home when I arrived and I just burst into tears. Also prevalent in my thoughts was the fact that it was my wedding anniversary and I couldn't believe that after a few years TF decided it was time to dispose of me and get a newer model (although 'model' and Slapper Features shouldn't really be used in the same sentence). The upside was that Jo-Jo's first tooth had come through! So, I drank wine with Mum, cried and celebrated my son's first tooth coming through. What a way to spend your wedding anniversary. Happy Anniversary Sarah!

Wednesday

TF came and was very cocky. I asked him if he wanted to see Jo-Jo at the weekend because he told me he wasn't able to come next week. Apparently he's busy this weekend as the rugby is on. He went to bath Jo-Jo and when he gave him his milk he didn't mention more dates at all. Then he went. No mention of when he'd phone to see how Jo-Jo was and I doubt whether he will. I think he likes a break at the weekend and it's an inconvenience for him to come down and see Jo-Jo. The rugby's on Saturday at 9.00am. Why couldn't he come on Sunday? It's not my fault he lives in Weston. I didn't ask him to have an affair and move away with Slapper Features. Ooh, I'm not feeling happy today! When I think of all the single Dads who climb up London Bridge dressed as Superman in protest at not having rights to see their children. I can't even get my estranged (although I feel just the word 'strange' is more befitting) husband to pick up the phone and find out how his son is. Arsehole!

Monday, December.

TF came. After our conversation last time about helping me at the weekends, he never mentioned it. I mentioned to him that we'd had a Christmas card from one of his TA friends. I told him I trusted he'd finally tell them the truth and stop telling people we hadn't been happy for a couple of years and thought that having a baby would bring us closer together. (Jo-Jo, if you ever read this my darling, I want you to know something. I would never have had a baby on the basis that it would bring me closer together with my partner. I wanted you out of love. It was an amazing experience carrying you and an unforgettable one having you! I'm sorry for what's happened with your father. I never expected him to do anything like this. You were brought to me and are the best thing that's ever happened to me. If it means dancing through the streets naked, I won't let you grow up with his morals. Although, debate of the year is, does he actually have any?)

Thursday.

TF was one hour late and just tried to walk in but I had put the chain on, the reason being that last week he just walked in and I was in the loo. I was so cross and when I reminded him I need my privacy he just sarcastically barked that this is half his house. However, today he banged his head on the glass because he didn't expect it to be locked. I found that very funny and made a mental note to do it again! He didn't say anything and didn't even apologise for being late. He then told me that he was reducing his monthly payments in accordance with government rules. He said he was going to use the rest to make a nursery for Jo-Jo. He's all bloody talk. He's never even mentioned about coming to see Jo-Jo alternate weekends. We discussed this over a week ago so does he think I'm stupid? He's just said that about the nursery because he doesn't want to pay me any more money. I couldn't care less about the money, it's Jo-Jo I feel sorry for.

Monday

TF came. I had to go up at bath time because Jo-Jo was crying. TF said he thought he'd just caught him with his watch. I told TF to cuddle his son but he still didn't stop crying. I cuddled Jo-Jo and he stopped. That felt good! I told TF I wasn't trying to be horrible but if he wants to build up a relationship with Jo-Jo he's got to see him more. He said he was getting himself sorted and it's taken a while. TF is coming to spend the afternoon with him on 22nd December and will give him his Christmas presents. I've decided

I've got to show him how to behave with Jo-Jo and what his likes/dislikes are because it upsets Jo-Jo and I don't suppose TF finds it easy. I just hope Slapper Features realises just what she's done to this family. It's our son's first Christmas and TF won't be here.

'Sod off' Saturday

TF came at 2.30pm to see Jo-Jo. He gave him a Christmas card and I told him it could go in his room because I didn't want it up. TF took it away and I did apologise later and explained that it was a difficult time for me. The card read 'Enjoy your first Christmas' and I wanted to shout out, you should have been here for it! Mum was here and we all got on okay, mainly for Jo-Jo. He didn't take him out because it wasn't very nice weather and he hadn't brought a car seat. He asked about seeing him over Christmas as he had a present for him. I told him to come whenever he wanted. We arranged 29th December. I told him he could take Jo-Jo for the whole day if he wanted and to come whenever he wants. I think Jo-Jo enjoys male contact and TF can give him a bit of 'rough and tumble'. We both said we'd sort something more permanent in the new year. I feel very strange about the whole situation. This will be my first Christmas without TF. It's such a good job we don't know what's around the corner.

Wednesday

Had an absolutely wonderful Christmas. Needless to say I was dreading it, but Mum and Jayne were there. I finished work on Christmas Eve and sat in the lounge with them in the afternoon watching a Christmas film. I wasn't looking forward to tomorrow at all. Bless him, Jo-Jo had a cold but I have to say, Mum Jayne and I did nothing but laugh. Jayne did her normal Christmas videoing and in every shot, apart from when we gave Jo-Jo a bath, there was either a glass of red wine, gin, Bacardi, or brandy in shot! If Jo-Jo ever watches it when he gets older he'll wonder how he survived as we were rather tipsy most of the time! On Boxing Day, after a couple of medicinal Bacardi's, I had the urge to knock down the Leaning Tower of Pisa that was our barbeque. Chris decided that he wanted to build his own when we moved in to the house and, well, it had more cement contained within the one hundred or so bricks than the whole of our house put together. It wasn't straight either, hence the nickname of Pisa! With every blow I vented my feelings and within minutes it was rubble. I was knackered and a bit dizzy from too much Bacardi, but pretending it was TF's head made the job so much easier! All in all a great Christmas, thanks to Mum and Jayne. Here's to a better new year for me, please.

Twat Face Tuesday

TF came and took Jo-Jo out. I asked when he was going to see him again and his idiot reply was 'haven't we got to wait to go to court to get the finances sorted?' What the hell did he mean by that and what's it got to do with seeing Jo-Jo? I told him he could come whenever he wanted and I've never stopped him. Again, he had no answer. I'm now realising that TF isn't very articulate and is actually quite thick! Mum and I gave Jo-Jo a Kit Kat finger, which he thoroughly enjoyed despite gagging on it. Mum panicked and I picked Jo-Jo up and patted him on the back. He cried but was absolutely fine. TF, with his vast medical background, amazed me because he didn't do anything to help. I feel the whole responsibility of Jo-Jo is on me. I then sat down and started peeling veg at the kitchen table when suddenly the silence was broken. . I had absolutely no idea this was coming and was quite taken aback.

'Are you happy with the way your life's turned out then Chris? Are you proud with what you've done?' The look of shock on my face was hilarious! I was peeling carrots and froze mid peel!

'I don't think that's a discussion I want to have in front of my son thanks Pauline'.

'I'm not raising my voice Chris, just asking you a question'.

'Again, I don't want this conversation in front of Johnathan thanks Pauline'.

'I treated you like a son Chris and you've let me down on a large scale'. Oh, I could have died on the spot. TF adopted the red and blotchy look on his face and neck and I carried on peeling a carrot that was practically all peel by now. When TF left Mum did apologise to me but it was just something she had to say. Jo-Jo is eight months old, he has no idea of what was being said so I don't know where TF was coming from to be honest. It was an excuse because he couldn't answer Mum's questions. Well done Mum, you go girl!

Saturday, January, 2004. (Can I start the year again please?)
I sold my wedding rings today as I need the money. What use are they to me now? Never again will I look down on people, or judge them, for having to sell, or pawn, things to get by. Although I never want TF back, it's still strange selling the rings I loved, rings that held so many memories of our time together. The engagement ring I picked all those years ago and the wedding ring TF put on my finger whilst looking at me with such love in his eyes. Oh and the eternity ring (or in TF's case the 'you'll do for now' ring). Hand made in Greece whilst we were on holiday with friends. Five gorgeous diamonds set in eighteen carat gold. All three rings looked beautiful on my finger and I was so proud of them. So, here I was, on show for the whole jeweller's shop to gossip about when I'd gone. I waited for the jeweller to inspect the rings to then only offer me £250 for all three. He looked embarrassed as I stared at him in desperation at the price he offered me. I accepted the money as I just wanted to get out of the shop because I could feel myself starting to break down. I will never forget today.

Sunday, February.

Chris dropped Jo-Jo back this evening after yet another day at the zoo. Jo-Jo will have been there so many times that by the time he's seven years old he'll be giving guided tours, have a lifetime membership and a seat named after him. I've had a really busy day so I just left his day bag on the kitchen table. What really annoys me is that Jo-Jo has been sick and I was just handed a bag of dirty clothes as if I was the hired help. Take them home and wash them you lazy gits! You're not doing me a favour Chris when you take our son out for the day. You're actually his Dad and need to deal with things that crop up (or spew out). Anyway, about fifteen minutes after dropping Jo-Jo back, Chris phoned me and sounded quite nervous, 'Erm, I'm on my way back, wont be long, I've left something in Johnathan's day bag.'

'Okay, see you in a bit', I said thinking bollocks, I've got to see you again. Ten minutes later, and I'm kicking myself now writing this, Chris turned up and asked for the day bag. I got it and he took out a camera! A bloody camera with photographic evidence of Slapper Features on it and everything! This was my perfect opportunity to see what she looked like. In the time it took him to come back, I could have done my impression of Tom Cruise in Mission Impossible, taken out the SD card, downloaded the photos onto the Internet and sent them off into the ether. Bloody hell Sarah, you donut! Apparently, according to TF's godmother, she's a rather large lady, some would say buxom, I prefer 'fat'. Apparently, she has unkempt, long black hair, enormous, pendulous boobs and according to my source he wasn't attracted by her looks. So, I've decided that from this point forward she will be known as Fat Bird!

Friday (Valentine's Day)

Oh, what a day, can't stop smiling and not because someone anonymous sent me a card or flowers, but because I had one over on Chris (*New Year, trying not to refer to him as Twat Face now, unless he truly deserves it).* Come to think of it, I've never had an anonymous card or flowers sent to me. I so wanted to be one of those girls walking to their car, or the bus, after a day at work with a gargantuan bouquet of flowers in her hand. Instead I was 'Billy no Boyfriend' doing the walk of shame to my car, empty handed, trying to stay positive...

So, Jayne and I decided Chris needed to think that someone fancied me. We hatched a cunning plan! One of her friends wrote me a card, which read, *Thank you for brightening up my day, all my love?* This wasn't any Valentine's Day card, this was a musical one! The point being that I would hook up the baby monitor in the nursery and have the listening device downstairs with me in the kitchen, listening intently to see if Chris fell into the trap whilst he was upstairs bathing Jo-Jo. I'd spent what seemed liked hours setting the card in just the right place. It needed to be in a position where he couldn't quite read it, so needed to turn it slightly. I whacked the volume on the baby monitor to 'full blast' on both units and waited impatiently in the kitchen for what seemed like hours. They moved into my bedroom so that Chris could dry Jo-Jo's hair. I heard him mumbling a few things to Jo-Jo, trying to talk baby talk, which just makes him sound even more thick than he is. Then it happened – *Isn't She Lovely* by Stevie Wonder came booming through the monitor. I heard Chris mutter 'shit' and I nearly cracked a rib laughing! He took a long time drying Jo-Jo's minimal hair and was very red when he came down. He didn't speak much to me and left very quickly. Oh I shall remember this for a long time!

Thursday, March.

I'm still trying to adjust to what's happened in my life and, quite frankly, I don't think I'm doing all that well today. I've just had a phone call with Chris about Jo-Jo in which he said the word 'we'. I wanted to pause him for a moment and take it all in. Whilst I would rather swim with hungry piranhas than take him back, I went all hot and my stomach churned at the mere mention of the word. How quickly he's accustomed to his new cosy little life.

'We will make sure he has a good time with us when he comes up', he said. If only it was possible to spit down a phone. I'm expected to get on with it now. He left me for Fat Bird and from this moment on it's 'we', 'us' and 'our'.

I hate her. I really, really hate her for what she's done to me. I have so many questions to ask her and so many things to say, 'What was the attraction of a married man?' 'When did Chris tell you I was pregnant?' 'This pregnancy was very much planned, despite what he may say.' 'I expect you find it hard to sleep at night knowing that an innocent baby is now going to grow up without his father at home because you couldn't keep your legs closed'. Oh I could go on but what would be the point? Isn't it strange how, one minute, you're with your husband, living together normally, laughing, joking, cuddling, having sex etc, and then, with the mere click of a finger almost, you can't stand the sight of each other. I'm shocked actually at just how quickly I've dismissed Chris out of my life. I cannot bear the sight of him; I can't look at him now and find it very hard to talk to him. I loved this man so very much and wanted to spend the rest of my life with him. Yet, as soon as he told me he was leaving me, my feelings towards him went from love to pure hate. Self-preservation maybe. I'm so glad my feelings have changed to hatred though, because I don't know how I would cope if I still loved him. I imagine that must be very hard to deal with.

Thursday
Chris will never cease to amaze me. I had a letter from a Building Society today advising that the house could now be 'let'. I had no idea what they were going on about. I phoned the Building Society to be told that Chris had instigated this. I phoned my solicitor who advised me not to worry as he'd received a letter as well with the suggestion of the house being let. Let? Let? Where

the hell am I supposed to live then Twat Face? Apparently, Chris had now received the inheritance from his late Mum's estate, £22,000! Yes that's £22,000. I'm shocked because I can't believe that Chris wouldn't even help me out with the mortgage, yet he's in receipt of a small blasted fortune, which, according to my solicitor, he's spent on a new car for Fat Bird (probably spent extra on a good suspension on the driver's side) paying off credit card debts and art! He wouldn't know art if it came up and said 'hello I'm art'.

Sunday (Mothers' Day)
Chris came today to take Johnathan out for the day. Bearing in mind it's my first Mother's Day, he came empty handed. A little bunch of flowers from Jo-Jo would have been appreciated and well received. He wanted to talk about finances and said that his solicitor had advised a clean break on both sides. I said that I had to sell the house I loved because of him and that if we hadn't gone for the extension, I wouldn't have to move. I told him I need all of the equity to re-house myself and Jo-Jo. I don't think he'll ever cease to amaze me, because he's offered to loan me money to pay for half of the mortgage. Loan me? What planet is he living on?

We exchanged many words and he left to take Jo-Jo out for the day. When Chris came back he was very quiet and said that he'd ring me about what we'd discussed. I said that unless he agreed to what I wanted then I'd see him in court. I hope this all gets sorted out soon as it's really beginning to affect me mentally and physically. I can't get to grips with it all. It's been six months now but I still feel as if I'm caught up in a tornado.

Saturday, April (Jo-Jo's first birthday)
Jo-Jo was one today. What a year it's been. I'm trying to get on with life but I think for a long time to come, his birthdays will bring me back to what happened with his birth and what Chris

did. Mum and I made a cake in the shape of a number 1 and iced it blue and covered it in Smarties. It looked lovely, even though I say so myself! A few of my friends came over with their small children and we had a little party for him. I held it together until 'Happy Birthday' was sung. The tears came then but I managed to dab them away onto a tissue and be strong (and have a glass of wine!). Jo-Jo seemed to have fun and enjoy all the attention he was receiving. I've got lots of photos to remind myself of the day that I wanted over and done with to be honest. Everyone was so kind and made me laugh, but we all knew it was a 'sad' day. I hope they're not always going to be like this. Bloody hell Sarah, cheer up girl!

Thursday, May. (I'm going on holiday, to a foreign land!)
Mum and Jayne have surprised me with a holiday to Majorca. I'm so excited. We're going in May. Sorted out passports for Jo-Jo and me today. I can't wait to feel some sun on me and have a change of scenery for a week. I've nothing to wear so need to have a spend. I'm so excited!

Sunday (Post holiday)
Hello Di, had a lovely holiday, even look a bit brown. The apartment was beautiful. The balcony was huge and Jo-Jo spent most of the time throwing a ball around it for me to bring back to him, for him to then throw it again etc etc. He took his first crawling steps as well, it was so sweet to see and he looked really pleased with himself. I am too, because that means he'll be walking soon and will be able to get things himself instead of sitting there, pointing at me and making a grunting noise! We spent a lot of time on the beach where Mum and Jayne made me relax whilst they took Jo-Jo off for a walk. It was heaven.

The sun shone as if making a special effort just for me. I loved being away. All I let myself think about was what we were going to do next, or what I should buy from the market. My life at home was a distant memory for a while. All three of us talked about what Chris had done and what we'd like to do with him. 'I want to tie the bastard to a chair and let him have some home truths about how he's let you down Sarah. One day he'll have a child with Fat Bird and understand exactly what he's put you through and left you with'. We'd had a few wines by this stage and Mum's tongue took no prisoners! Now that I'm home I can feel myself getting irritable and tense again at the thought of having no one to share the responsibility of Jo-Jo with me. It's been so nice to have someone to take him off my hands for a bit and give me some mental peace and quiet. Back to reality and the house filled with sadness, stress, depression and memories of Chris.

Sunday, June.
Chris was due to pick Jo-Jo up at 10.30am. He phoned me at 10.20am to say he'd forgotten to put the car seat in and had to go back. For the love of God man, all you have to remember is the car seat. He suggested that he now bring him back at 7.30pm and he could have his tea at his house. I didn't like this idea so said that he could give him his tea at mine because I knew Chris had moved in May but didn't know where. So when he takes Johnathan out I have no idea where he is. What I couldn't get through to him was how irresponsible would I look to the authorities if I said I just let my son go out with his father but didn't have a clue where he lived or where he was taking him. Also, what if something happened to me and the police or someone needed to get to Chris's house? Chris may be Jo-Jo's father but he's no parent. When he last saw Jo-Jo he knew that he was taking him to Somerset. All he had to say was, 'Look Sarah, this is our new address and would you mind if I take Johnathan back to our house?' I would have been fine with this, worried sick but fine. Jo-Jo is still only fourteen months old after all. We have years ahead of this and I wish Chris would speak to me. I'm not bitter about him and his life. I'm a great believer in fate and

I'm looking forward to my own future. He's put me through a lot of stress and upset me over the last nine months and I've coped really well. I even found Chris's christening confirmation card the other day in the loft and gave it to him. I don't really think I ever knew him you know. However, we both have to realise that we need to discuss things about Johnathan and all I'm asking for is for him to be honest with me and to stop trying to hurt me with unkind and unnecessary words and actions. I never asked for any of this, or indeed deserve it.

Tuesday Letter from Chris. Tosser. What did we have in common? I doubt my own mind to be honest because he truly is an arse!

Sarah, further to our telephone conversation in relation to my access to Johnathan, I feel compelled to express my views in writing. I have taken the advice of my solicitor and confirm my address as above. You have my mobile number as a point of contact. My solicitor sees no reason why you should need my home phone number. Also, as we will not always be at home with Johnathan, my mobile number would be the best to contact me on. If there is a cost issue, I will call you back.

I appreciate you feel that I should have mentioned to you that I was taking Johnathan to Somerset. However, you had previously accepted him going out of Torbay, thus I did not see this as a problem. Also, the original agreement was made at a time when I was living in Weston-super-Mare and had just started living with Mary and as such it made sense. I also did not see the point in collecting Johnathan, driving an hour and a half up the M5 for a few hours at the house to only have to drive back again. Certainly not my idea of quality time for Johnathan and I. However, Mary and I now live in our own house in Wellington and when buying the house we took into consideration Johnathan's needs. He will be safe and comfortable here.

In relation to my Thursday evening visits, I can understand your feelings that you do not wish me to enter your new home when you move. However, I fail to understand why, all of a sudden, after seven months of visits you are unable to allow me to continue to see

Johnathan. I wish to continue these visits until you are able to move. I anticipate this will not be for at least eight months. I feel that the continuation of these visits, along with weekend access, will help ease Johnathan towards being able to say overnight with us. Surely, as you pointed out, it is what is best for Johnathan and I feel this is the best way forward.

Whilst writing, I feel we should also discuss access at Christmas. You are aware that I feel Johnathan should spend alternate Christmas times with us. This time should be from Christmas Eve through to the day after Boxing Day. As you do not feel that Johnathan is yet ready to spend time overnight with me, I trust it is not a problem for me to collect him on Christmas Day, returning later in the evening, this year. Following your comments the other day, I have purchased a pushchair/ buggy to go with the highchair and travel cot we have already purchased. As you quite correctly point out, we both want what is best for Johnathan and believe me I have his best interests at heart. I hope that, for Johnathan's sake, we are able to amicably agree over these issues.

Chris.

We, us, our, blah blah blah. Mary this, Mary that. Sod off Chris and 'Fat Bird Mary Bit Tits'. I have PMT so not in the mood for his bilge. Off to open wine.

Thursday

I phoned my solicitor for some advice on the 'orders' I've received from the happy couple. We agreed that Chris's mobile number would be sufficient contact. Chris wants Johnathan alternate Christmases. My view is that why doesn't he want to see more of him on bank holidays or even Easter? Forget the religious aspects, it's a four day holiday. Christmas is my special time with Johnathan. I've had the ups and downs all year, the sleepless nights, the guilty feelings because I have to leave him at nursery whilst I earn a wage, the tantrums, projectile vomit, etc

etc. I have all that to cope with *on my own*. Why should Chris have the lovely times? It was his choice to leave.

I phoned Chris and had a chat. I cried because he couldn't see why he couldn't come to see Johnathan on a Thursday. I couldn't get across to him that I feel very uncomfortable and feel like my privacy is being invaded. I find it very difficult to keep myself away for two hours and don't see why I should feel like that in my own home. I've been through a hell of a lot over the last few months and think I've been very accommodating. I always offer him a drink and try and chat but I can't emotionally cope with it anymore. Some women cut up clothes, change the locks. Hell, I heard that one woman put posters up all over her local town naming and shaming her adulterous husband and said that she's seen bigger willies on new born babies. What happened to the caring and considerate man I knew? I'm dreading Sunday, absolutely dreading it, because he's taking Johnathan up to Wellington.

Friday, July. (Release Day)
Got this in the post today – free, free at last!

Dear Sarah
I enclose your decree absolute of divorce dated 1st July. This is the final divorce decree. It ends your marriage to Chris. Please keep this document in a safe place as you will need to produce it to the Registrar should you wish to re marry in the future. I draw your attention to the note on the decree, which explains the impact of divorce upon inheritance under a will.
   Yours sincerely
   Richard
   GRW Solicitors

Being honest now Di, I read this letter when I got home from work last night, and just filed it safely for future reference. Is that weird? I'm so intent on getting on with my life and coming to terms that my past in the rear view mirror (it's small and all you can see is what's happened and if you look in it too much you'll crash and burn) and the future is the windscreen. It's big and I'm looking ahead whilst surveying all that comes my way.

Chapter 6

Going Solo

Keep steadily before you the fact that all true success depends at last upon yourself.
Theodore T. Hunger

Tuesday, August.

I've had to cancel life insurance policies to help pay the bills. Went shopping with Mum at the weekend and I know I'm so near to my overdraft limit that I was positively shaking because I was convinced my card wouldn't go through. The relief on my face must have been so obvious but Mum didn't say anything. I've always been brought up to 'save for a rainy day' and right now I'm flooded. From the day I started work I always had money. I loved going out for a spend, buying clothes and have wild nights out on the town, without a care in the world. Now I was constantly in the 'red' and praying that I wouldn't reach my overdraft limit, which in itself is rather large. How the hell did I end up here? Before all of this happened, I used to look at people's trolleys with 'own' brand items and think yuck, I'd never buy that, how embarrassing. I no longer judge because that person buying 'own' brand food is now me.

Friday

Great, I feel like wearing a painted black cross on my forehead indicating that I'm not even able to pay for my own prescriptions now, just received an exemption card. Whilst it's bloody fab I don't have to pay, it's just more proof that I'm poor! Usually you just discretely tick the box, but sometimes a locum chemist will bellow out, 'Do you pay for your prescription!' I shake my head. Chemist shouts again 'Okay, tick the appropriate box to indicate why you don't have to pay.' At this point, I can feel everyone pause what they're doing and turn to me, assuming, single Mum, tax credits, sponger. I have been so tempted to explain why I don't pay, which is silly really. I feel I have to justify my reasons. Stupid, I know as it's none of their business.

Thursday

I hate the mechanical world and whilst I'm gaining confidence, I seem to turn into a gibbering wreck when I walk into a tyre shop. I have a brilliant mechanic, but he doesn't do tyres so I had to go to somewhere 'foreign' today and hated it. In this 'strange' garage they mumbled the words drive it on to the ramp love and we'll take a look. Do they not know how difficult it is to do this as a woman? Not because we can't drive, but because we know everyone will be looking at us to fail and either drive off the other side of the ramp or miss it altogether. I walked very confidently to my car and did a small sign of the cross on my chest. And yes, they were all looking at me. Thank God I made it. Slight over rev on the entrance to the ramp but overall pretty good. Getting out of the working area thing wasn't quite so good, as I slipped on some oil and skidded. I then had to wait in the reception area whilst the mechanic asked me which tyres I was going for. How the fuck would I know I thought. 'Well, I do a lot of mileage annually and need good quality ones please. The last lot I had went on the trim too quickly'. I had absolutely no idea what I was talking about but I'm not into girly giggling and pleading ignorance anymore. The waiting area is very male dominated in these places and the magazines all geared around men. I was the only female there and tried to look confident and put on an air of 'don't mess with me'. Then the bloke said, 'All done love, you can drive it off now and park outside'. What? You want me to reverse off the ramp, steer clear of the stack of old tyres that look as if they'll fall at the slightest nudge, and miss the big gaping hole that my car could quite easily fall into? I was 'walking the green mile' and took a mental picture of all obstacles in my path, memories of my driving test countless years ago coming to haunt me. I did it! I knew I could, but perhaps not at the speed they would have done it. Two metaphorical fingers duly stuck up to them before I drove off with my lovely new tyres! Who is the new woman? Where has this new found confidence come from?

Fit to Flop Friday

How am I? I hear you ask. In a word – knackered. I know my secretarial job isn't hard but it's mentally tiring and I'm the sort of person who needs just half an hour to myself when I get in from work to simply unwind. I picked Jo-Jo up from nursery tonight to be told that he'd had a three hour sleep at lunch time and probably won't be tired tonight Mummy. Thanks a sodding lot. I'll ring you up when he's still awake at 9.00pm shall I and ask for your advice. I pay you a small fortune on a daily basis and he sleeps for half the bloody day. Come 6.30pm all I'm thinking about is a glass of wine and evening telly. Not happy.

Monday, September.

I knew yesterday was going to be difficult, but I've got to get used to the fact that I'm going to have so many episodes in my life where I'll be thinking, I can't believe I'm doing this on my own, we should be doing this as a family. Again, me being me, I give myself two choices. I either go down hill or not. I'm choosing the latter. Whilst it's not proving to be very easy, I'm determined not to take a wrong turn and end up on 'Doom Street'. Jo-Jo's christening was at 11.00am and I was more than determined to look my best for this event. I didn't know if Fat Bird was coming at this point, I would have been very surprised if she was, but even so, I'm the Mum so will always have the upper hand. Our side of the family is relatively small but I'd invited friends too as I needed lots of moral support. Chris and his 'team' were waiting in the tea shop but I saw him stride out and walk towards me. 'I want to take Johnathan inside to see the family.' I didn't mind, but wouldn't have had much choice as he just took him off me. He'd not been gone five minutes and I could hear him crying (Jo-Jo not Chris!). I feel like a sheep who can hear her lamb bleating in the next field. Without any hesitation I walk into the tea room.

'I'll take him thanks, he obviously wants me.' I whisked him out of Chris's arms and took him back to his proper family. I didn't notice if Fat Bird was there. I'm sure she wasn't as although I didn't clock who was there, I'm sure I'd have noticed her unkempt hair and boobs you could rest a pint on. I didn't choose the best day for a christening as it was some special service, which seemed to last forever. Jo-Jo was getting bored and kept blowing raspberries at the Vicar. Not good! For even the most unobservant person, it was pretty obvious our two families were divided. Not even the strong incense swung around by the Vicar could penetrate the atmosphere between the two camps. The church isn't that big so we had to sit opposite each other unfortunately. Mum had 'the look' on her all throughout the service. It was the one she reserved for Jayne and I as children when we knew we'd over stepped the mark and been naughty. However, it was Chris's turn today!

'Chris and Sarah have brought Johnathan Albert James into the world and promise to look after him.' The Vicar's words seemed pointless. What an absolute farce this is. We may have brought him to the world 'Vic' but one of us has cocked up big time, and it ain't me! Mum kept giving me concerned looks whilst holding back tears, which then nearly tipped me over the emotional edge. Chris's brother is the first godfather to promise to look after my Jo-Jo. I so want to pause things right now and say something like You promise to look after my son? You're just as spineless as your brother. Having affairs and leaving wives must run in your family. Your Dad did it, you did it, more than once, and now Chris has done it. Yet you stand here in front of a

Vicar and promise to be a good godfather. I'd be more confident in Fred and Rosemary West's ability quite frankly.

So, after a few empty and meaningless promises from Chris's family and fought back tears from my side, that was it. Jo-Jo's christening over and done with. I felt numb, went home and got very drunk with my family! The afternoon far excelled the morning. It turned into a party. Perhaps not what one would normally expect of a christening, but then Jo-Jo's christening was never going to be conventional was it. My friends and family were so kind and did everything they could to make it a happy one for me. There were twelve of us around my dining room table eating the chilli and casserole I'd make the night before, drinking wine and laughing. Jo-Jo sat in his highchair at the table with us and decided he'd quite like to dip his fingers in my red wine and have a taste! Typical of my family, he enjoyed it and went in for more, this time trying to pick up the glass! That's my boy. 'A toast to Johnathan on his christening day. God bless you my darling and may you have a long and happy life' Mum said and we all chinked glasses and drank more wine. She'd bought him a beautiful christening cake and I had lots of photos taken with him for the album. All in all a good day, but I'm glad that hurdle's been cleared. On to the next one, whatever it may be.

Tuesday, November.
Jo-Jo and I snuggled up on the sofa tonight with his last bottle of warm milk, jarmies on, bunny dunny and C 'bloody' Beebies. Don't get me wrong, great programme, but it's not aimed at my age group and the same programmes at bedtime hour do get incredibly monotonous. He loves Balamory and squeals with delight when it's on. I've grown to hate the obnoxious woman who runs the nursery because at the end of every episode she waves to us as she enters her quiet, baby free and stress free, home. She can go out if she wants to, or stay in and watch television in peace. Then, she'll totter off to bed and have a good

night's sleep and wake up refreshed in the morning. What worries does she have? None. Bitch. Anyway, to pass the boredom I've made up my own version of the goodnight song. I sing it to Jo-Jo who hasn't got a clue what I'm saying and you know what, it makes me feel so much better...

The time has come to say goodnight
to say sleep tight, cos the day's been 'shite'.
Oh the time has come to say goodnight
at the end of a boring day.
I've not had much fun today,
tomorrow's just another day.
And now it's time to say goodnight
at the end of a dreary day.

Jo-Jo now cries when it's over, mind you so do I, but mine's sheer relief that the bilge has finished. Have come to the conclusion I'm not a natural Mum. What do you think Di?

Saturday, December.
I have discovered a secret channel on the television. I'm fed up with constant reminders of Chris on the radio and television. It's silly little things like cereal adverts (the ones I used to buy for him). I came across Classic FM TV. It's been part of my life for two weeks now. When Jo-Jo is having his nap, I make myself sit down and close my eyes and just be, if that makes sense. There are no reminders of my previous life with Chris. It's all new music and it's mine. Sarah's new world where it's invitation only to enter and no twats allowed.

I've not told anyone about it, except you Di, because I don't want anyone else to tarnish it. I'm in love with a song by Elton John and Pavarotti, 'Live Like Horses'. It makes me feel alive and realise that I can be free, not just of Chris but of the feelings of irritability, guilt, and anxiety, to name but a few.

Tuesday, February, 2005.

I need to do something to stop my head exploding. I'm going to bed worrying about everything and anything. Last night, I was worried about Jo-Jo starting school, in two years. Then I keep worrying about money, how I'm going to cope, what I need to do tomorrow, going over arguments I've had with Chris and analysing things I've said to friends. I'm worrying that I've upset them, when I know I haven't, but I just can't stop having these thoughts. That straight jacket will soon become a reality if I'm not careful.

Thursday, March.

I'm still not right. I don't want to talk to anyone sometimes, especially in the evenings. I hate it when the phone rings. Just lately, I've been hearing voices in my head. Things like, 'you've done something wrong at work', 'something major is going to go wrong with your car' and 'you've left the iron on and it's burning the house down right now'. I can convince myself that someone's talking about me. I don't like it when this happens. It was Gill's hen night at the weekend. She'd arranged for about forty of us to go out for a meal. I was sat with her friends and mainly people I didn't know. I used to be the life and soul of the party and would chat to everyone and anyone, including strangers going to and fro from the toilet. On this occasion though I just wanted to run as I could feel my head struggling to stay on my shoulders. I knew Gill's friends must be thinking I was very rude because I had a face like thunder and wasn't joining in with the celebrations, but I couldn't cope with being there. Everyone was happy and enjoying themselves and all seemed to have perfect lives, money and no worries. One of the worst nights for me since Chris left.

Sunday

Went to Gill's 'evening do' last night and was forced to dance and put a smile on my face, but I felt everyone was looking at me and talking about me, saying horrible things about the way I looked. They probably were talking about me to be honest and saying things like, 'Miserable cow, look at the face on that.' I also felt they knew my situation. They obviously didn't, but I think paranoia is setting in a bit. I was forced to dance and look happy. I'd bought new shoes and the soles weren't being nice to me, so I kept slipping. I looked like I was trying to do my 'robotic' dancing from yonder year. Normally, I would have laughed and dramatised things, but last night, truth be told, I wanted to pause everyone, scream very loudly, cry, and get pissed. Something's not right and 'girl power' is not as strong as it was. I've never been like this.

Wednesday

Last night, I tried out my new technique of how to relax when I go to bed. I've put a pad on the cabinet by me to write down things that are worrying me. If it all gets too much when I'm trying to sleep and my thoughts take over, I write everything down on a pad and it's immediately out of my head. It seems to work, but I need an A4 pad, as it's obvious I have a lot that worries me. Some nights a flipchart would be useful.

Thursday, May.

Smudge went today. I feel like the worst person in the world. My finances are getting worse and so I've had to make cut backs. The Blue Cross said they'd take both of the cats and find them a new home together, but Shanie died a couple of months ago after being attacked by some thug looking cat. I took her to the vets and she said that the kindest thing I could do was put her out of her misery. I feel very guilty because I didn't really have time to say goodbye to her. I cried more when she died than I did when Chris left. Smudge hasn't been himself and was getting pissed off with Jo-Jo's high-pitched scream and his attempts at stroking him, which, to Smudge, must have felt like a jack hammer on his head. So, I had the call today from The Blue Cross to say that they had a space for him. It caught me by surprise and I was cooking Jo-Jo's lunch at the time. I couldn't stop shaking. Barbara looked after Jo-Jo for me and I put Smudge in his cat basket. I held it together until I got there. The centre manager gave me a disapproving look, which didn't do much for the feelings of guilty I was having. I had to fill out a form and sign Smudge over to the centre. 'Why are you giving Smudge away Mrs Chilton?' 'Because my husband left me a few months ago with a baby to look after and I just can't afford to keep him any longer. It's breaking my heart to do it but I don't have any choice.' Her attitude changed then and she felt sorry for me. It still doesn't stop me from feeling crap. Sorry not good company tonight. I just miss my cats.

Monday, August.
Moving to a two bed-roomed, semi-detached house in a new housing estate tomorrow. It's lovely and is at the end of a cul-de-sac. It has a kitchen/diner and a lounge on the ground floor and two bedrooms, ensuite for me if you please, and a bathroom upstairs. Taking into account what I've left, this is going to be quite an adjustment for me, however it will be mine with no memories of Chris in it. Right now I'm in Jo-Jo's bedroom. He's asleep and oblivious to everything. When I think about all Chris and I have done to this house, and how I longed for my big kitchen and utility room, Jo-Jo's nursery is the room I shall miss for a long long time, possibly forever.

This is the room I painted whilst heavily pregnant. I had to keep sitting down to rest because I knew I'd over done it, but Chris was at work and I was panicking that we wouldn't get it all done. Well, he probably wasn't at work was he, but off shagging Fat Bird. Anyway, this room is where I sat when it was all newly furnished and daydreamed about what sort of Mum I was going to be and imagining what our child would look like. I sat here the day I left hospital, still dazed from the anaesthetic and numb from what I'd just been through, trying to breastfeed this little man and no clue how to do it. This room has witnessed laughter, tears, both mine and Jo-Jo's, anxiety, worry, excitement and so much more. If I had one pound for every time I've peered through the crack in the door to spy on Jo-Jo to see if he's either sleeping, or to just watch him, I'd have paid my mortgage off I think. Thanks to Mum, the corner of the room was constantly stacked with nappies and wet wipes and newly purchased clothes where she said 'I saw this and could just see him in it'. Oh Di, I want to bottle this room and take it with me. I'm feeling quite maudlin this evening and I've not even had any wine! I'll be okay, but it's weird to think that I'll never see this room again.

Wednesday, October.
Evening Di, all went well with the move. I'm growing accustomed to the small lounge, which I swear is getting smaller each day. Jo-Jo seems to love his new bedroom and has adapted very well to the move. I've taken a few days off to have the windows changed to double-glazing. The original ones were pretty crap to be honest. Anyway, the reason I'm writing is to have a rant and a little 'praise Sarah' time. The window company are in full flow installing lovely new windows for me. so I decided to pop out for a bit of retail therapy. Well, when I say retail therapy, I wish I meant bags and bags of lovely clothes with matching handbags and jewellery. I don't. I needed a new pair of jeans and that's about all I can afford at the moment. I couldn't work out which pair of jeans to try so I took all six into the changing room! I need to diet by the way. It's not very often you get a 360 degree look of yourself. Anyway, I was just trying to peel off the skinny fit jeans and was beginning to sweat a little, and at the same time deeply regretting the decision to try them on, when I overhead a conver-

sation between two assistants. They were talking about single mothers so that immediately got my attention and I transformed into a meerkat in the changing room, straining to hear them.

Ass one: ('ass' being quite appropriate), 'We have single Mums in our road, they get on my nerves, pushing their prams round all day, sponging off the state. They should be made to go out and get a job'.

Ass two: 'I agree. They're all on benefits and make no effort to get a job and it's people like us who pay taxes, paying for them to stay at home all day and do nothing'.

I turned from an inquisitive meerkat to a raging bull! I changed back to my own clothes and could feel myself shaking and breathing erratically. I composed myself as best I could before I went in for the kill. Being a redhead I tend to fly off the handle and say things without thinking so I knew I needed to compose myself first. I casually and calmly walked up to them, big smile on my face so that they'd think I was asking for a different size, lull them into a false sense of security.

'Hi there. Was it you and your colleague who were just talking about single Mums? I couldn't help but overhear in the changing room.' Ass 1 was taken aback and mumbled a pathetic acknowledgement. Ass two looked over too so I had their full attention. Good! 'I'm a single Mum and I took great offence at what you were saying. My husband left me when our son was five months old for a woman he'd been having an affair with for eighteen months. I didn't ask to be in this position and I'm finding it very hard. I work for a living and don't sponge off the state as you so eloquently put it. Don't judge people. You should be ashamed of yourselves and should keep these naïve and immature conversations for the staff room'. At that point I could feel the tears welling up inside me, but at the same time could smell the fear coming from Ass one and Ass two. I went to pay for my jeans and kept staring at them. I went out a bit shaky, but was inwardly singing Aretha Franklin's R.E.S.P.E.C.T!

Friday

Still waking up in the night, but am now telling myself to stop worrying. I'm sleeping a lot better now. What I've also learnt is that when I read back what I've written down in the night in my obvious panic, I could almost laugh at in the morning. Last week I wrote, must mow the lawn (garden not mine!). For the love of all that is Cadbury's Sarah, get a life and stop worrying about mowing the bloody lawn. So, I actually tell myself that now and I can feel my head starting to relax and I get a good night's sleep.

Chapter 7

Snow White and the Seven Dwarfs Part I

(A guide to Internet dating for delusional optimists.)

A man on a date wonders if he'll get lucky. The woman already knows.
Monica Piper

Thursday, October, 2005.
That's it, enough is enough, I have decided to try and find a man. My evenings are boring and I need to do something to get myself out of this rut. Trigger point number one was last night when I shouted obscenities at the video machine for not recording *Neighbours*. Secondly, when I actually cried about it because I needed to know if Harold's dog made it through surgery. After regaining composure and reminding myself that it's just a programme and the dog was acting, I have decided to find something constructive to do of an evening. I couldn't think of anything meaningful so decided to try out the 'wonderful' world of Internet dating.

My favourite site has a section that asks Would you like to meet this man? It gives you 3 boxes to click on; yes, no or maybe. Well I have decided the site needs to add more options, so I propose the following, even if it's just for my benefit. And my extended options are:

1. Not with a 10ft bargepole.
2. Maybe after a trip to the dentist, barber and plastic surgeon.
3. Maybe if he grows by at least a foot.
4. Is that male?
5. Hell will freeze over before I entertain that idea.

6. Would rather shave my own head.
7. May entertain the idea for charity.
8. Not with that wallpaper

Friday
Karl1968 has sent me a message again to say hi. Not bad looking, only one photo. Have come to the conclusion, very quickly, to avoid men with names like 'sexy69', 'bigdick' and 'pussylicker'. I have standards and a small child and that's just gross.

Tuesday (Never mind Mr Right, I need Mr Right Now.)
This Internet dating thing is addictive. I cannot go a day without logging on to see who's emailed me. It's becoming a ritual now. I put Jo-Jo to bed, clear up downstairs and ensconce myself in my 'dating den'. I hope I don't take it too seriously and start printing off photos of my potential suitors and plaster them all over my study wall, to be taken down and ritualistically burnt if they ignore my advances!

Thursday
Encountered my first bona fide arsehole this evening. He's a plumber. Not bad looking. He sent me a chat message, which just said *Hi Sarah, watcha?* God I hate that word, so lazy. He even put three kisses after it.

'Have you met anyone on here yet then Sarah? Xxx'

The trick is to leave it a few minutes before you reply. Don't seem too keen.

'No one special, I've only just joined. How about you?'

'I've met a couple but quite frankly some of you women on here are fucking weirdxxx'.

Nice.

'Well you must be a little hopeful at finding someone otherwise you wouldn't be on this site. Perhaps you're talking to the wrong women?'

'Yeah and that probably includes you you ugly bitch'. PS, do your collars and cuffs match?'

Charming. I couldn't actually speak for a while and could feel an asthma attack coming on. I don't have asthma so this was rather worrying. Where the hell did that outburst come from? I eventually calmed down.

'Oh dear, not good at this communication thing are you. Truth be told you're not intelligent enough to have a conversation with, and you're obviously a very bitter man. It may help if you have your hair cut and, more importantly, washed, and a trip to the dentist is clearly long overdue. As regards my 'collars and cuffs' as you so eloquently put it, they do match, but with your lack of charm and looks I'm surprised you've ever been invited to check any out'.

He didn't reply to me! I felt very smug (and drunk) after this and decided that I really ought to have a very large glass of water as I could feel myself shrivelling up with dehydration from the 'medicinal' wine I was forced to drink by 'knob head'.

I went to bed with the satisfaction that I'd put a very rude man in his place

Tuesday
Still communicating with Karl1968 and have also developed a new obsession with the who's looked at me page. But the downside to that is that you see someone gorgeous who's viewed you, you like their profile but they never make contact. That could potentially affect one's confidence, so I try to avoid looking at that icon. Back to Karl whose photo looks okay, he's a strawberry blonde and 6ft, nice face, kind, but isn't smiling very much. It was obviously a photo he'd taken himself on his phone. We've chatted a few times on line. He's got a little girl who's a couple of years older than Jo-Jo. His wife had an affair three years ago and

left him and he is now ready to date again. We've exchanged numbers and I'm meeting him for lunch on Sunday. What shall I wear?

Saturday
I have a date with Karl tomorrow. Why me? Why do I do this? I threw my entire wardrobe on the bed this morning to see what I can wear. Oh God, what am I going to wear? It's been such a long time since I've had to think about this. And breathe.

Sunday (Goofy)
Sarah, you are never to do this again. If you ever think of dating someone else read this first. You have been warned my girl! It was a glorious day, not a cloud in the sky; however, inside my stomach there was a storm brewing! I'd not spoken to Karl at all but he phoned me this morning to arrange where to meet. I should have heard the alarm bells ringing over his rather camp voice. I put the phone down after having arranged to meet him in the most public and open space known to man, and sat on the bed and thought oh God, why am I doing this, I'm about to meet Julian-bloody-Carey. I went for the casual look, jeans and slightly flirty, revealing cross over top. I decided to reveal my assets to detract from the liability around my middle and went for a flat shoe. I don't like heels very much, I always get them stuck in the blasted pavement.

I was meeting Karl at 1.00pm and the drive would take me approximately twenty minutes. I left at 12.00pm. I need to work on this OCD thing about being early, it's just ridiculous. I wish I'd never left at all. I had to allow for endless 'final' visits to the toilet before I left. I'd forgotten there was so much involved in dating. I had to plan my route to allow for an emergency toilet stop and I knew there was a toilet in Morrisons on the way so if I really had an overwhelming urge to go I could make a Starsky and Hutch entrance in the car park, roll over the bonnet, abandon the car, leaving all doors open and run in. All I needed was the Colt 45 in my hand to make my entrance look as if it warranted such dramatics.

I arrived with thirty-five minutes to spare and felt the need to do an SAS style 'reckie' of where to wait for him. Do I stand nonchalantly propped up against a lamp post, or sit casually on a bench? If sitting on a bench, do I read a magazine, or pretend to be texting someone? All these things needed to be considered. I went for the nonchalantly sitting on a bench whilst pretending to text someone. I now wish I'd opted for 'waiting in car with engine running'. I kept seeing men and thought Oh God is that him? Please don't say that's him. Even though I'd seen a photo of Karl, I was still wondering what he really looked like.

I was trying so hard to look relaxed, but inside I was a volcano waiting to erupt. A middle aged couple walked by me holding hands and I thought Lucky bastards, they've done the courting thing and are now relaxed with each other and have got all the awkwardness out of the way. I wish I was them right now. Shortly after, I was doing my nonchalant scan of the area, and this man was walking towards me. He was looking at me so I assumed it was Karl. For that split second it was okay and then he smiled and said hello. I was meeting the Mad Hatter. His two front teeth were huge! I wanted to scream why didn't you have a smiling photo on your profile you thoughtless bastard. I needn't have put myself through this if you had.

He kissed me on the cheek and I could feel his teeth. Yuck. Oh it was torture. We chatted and I was smiling at this point and being so nice but I just wanted to distract him and run like the wind. Give credit where it's due, he smelt gorgeous, but I just couldn't help wishing he was someone else. We walked to the restaurant and I asked for a diet coke but needed a bottle of house rose, find a corner seat and get pissed. The pub was lovely, a little wine bar type place. Jazz music, which I hate, but I didn't feel that was a good enough excuse to leave unfortunately. I was so tense with Karl I could feel cramp setting in.

We then ordered lunch. I wanted the easiest thing to eat on the menu and nothing that could a: potentially leave something in my teeth, b: squirt c: be too hot where you feel your whole face burn but are out in public and can't spit it out, so have no option but to swallow it and it feels like burning anthracite. The conversation wasn't great. At 2.00ish I decided enough was enough. I didn't have the heart to tell him I'd been bored shitless. Karl duly paid and we left the restaurant. There was no way in hell I was hanging around to give him the opportunity for a kiss! We walked to where we first met. You could have driven a mini between us. 'Well thanks for lunch Karl and it was nice to meet you'.

'You too Sarah, give me a call some time if you fancy going out again'

'Yes, definitely, bye Karl'.

Definitely? Definitely? What the hell did I say that for? I got back to my car, slumped over the steering wheel and vowed never to do this again.

Tuesday (Twitcher)

This one's different, I can just feel it. I have been chatting to Simon for a while. He plays the violin and teaches in schools. Divorced. No children. Photo not that clear but the legs are good enough for me! His voice was really masculine when we spoke, yet soft and sexy and a Yorkshire accent. I am now going to bed thinking of that gorgeous voice. I have good vibes about Simon. Could he be the one?

Thursday, November.

I was meeting Simon at 7.30pm last night. He arrived literally two minutes after me in a rather disappointing car. An Escort, newish model, but I'm more of a snob than I thought. As soon as I saw him in the car, but I did think she shoots she scores. He got out and said hello in that gorgeously sexy voice that just made me melt. I was smitten within the first thirty seconds. Really good looking, lovely face, opened the pub door for me, bought me a drink. We sat opposite each other and started talking. He was leaning on the table and obviously trying to get close to me. He was telling me about his day. He taught the violin to school children during the day and was moaning about the head teacher not providing him with enough time to teach.

'So, basically, they've employed me to teach music to the kids and I feel my talents are wasted there. I'm part of an orchestra but this pays good money, but they just need to give me more time to do what I do really well'. I have to say that I wasn't in the slightest bit interested, but listened intently to what he was saying as I was also trying to 'suss him out'. Simon didn't really ask much about me and it was beginning to annoy me a bit, but I was telling myself to not be so quick to judge and to take into account for obvious nerves.

Then, out of nowhere, a twitch appeared. I could feel myself gasp out loud and jump back in shock because it frightened the life out of me! His eyes squinted and he pulled back his lips over his mouth as if he wanted to show me his teeth. He did it again! This was after talking about his ex wife for most of the night and telling me how she had been in the same orchestra as him and she had an affair with his friend. This was also after he announced that he'd left his violin in the car and had better bring it in as it is worth £5,000. Oh Why me? Why me? He came back with his violin, which looked more like the size of a guitar. For some obscure reason though, I liked him. I bought us a second drink, but made Simon go to the bar and get it. He had a nice bum and I have the habit of doing a nervous walk if I think someone's looking at me.

We left just after last orders and did that dreaded walking to the car thing that I absolutely hate! 'Thanks Sarah for a lovely evening. Would you like to meet again?' he asked.

'Yes that would be lovely,' I said with my best smile. I kissed Simon on the cheek 'Great, well then I'll text you'. Apart from that awful twitch thing, the date had gone well. He talked about himself more than I would have liked, I didn't really need to know about how many times they tried to have children or that he read Caravan Monthly when trying to give a sperm sample. However, I was looking beyond the faults and trying to think positively. I drove home with a big smile on my face. It was so nice to have had male company and I blasted out some dance music in the car, as I felt alive again. Someone fancies me and it's given me such a boost of confidence.

Friday
Simon and I have been texting a lot. I love receiving texts, seeing the little envelope when you look at your phone. It's as if it's saying to you 'quick, you've got a message. You are wanted!'

Sunday (Text Fatigue)
Getting annoyed with Simon's texts now as ninety nine per cent of them are just so pointless. I took Jo-Jo to see Noddy yesterday with a couple of friends. Simon sent me a text to see how I was and what I was doing. I told him where I was and he texted back to say give Big Ears his love. Five minutes later I had one asking if I had seen Noddy yet. Oh my God, stop bugging me with crap Simon, you're becoming slightly too intrusive for my liking. However, it is so nice to think that I'm probably part of a real couple now and have a boyfriend! It's reassurance that someone likes me, that I am worthy.

Wednesday
I was more relaxed driving to meet Simon this time. I was really looking forward to it. I'd dressed a little bit more revealingly as well; cross over top that was a little bit lower than I would have normally dared to wear. What a tart and on the second date as

well! Simon had arrived first and this time we met in the public car park opposite. I obviously parked next to him (hoping that I didn't actually crash my car into his). I tried to look nonchalant, but deep down was thinking, God he really is gorgeous. He gave me a kiss on the cheek and bought me a drink. Again, he looked, and smelt, gorgeous. That lovely fresh 'just out of the shower' smell. My mind was being very dirty at this time and I was having a lovely time in my head! It was all perfect apart from that bloody twitch.

The evening was going so well, body language (and twitch) a bit more relaxed. I was leaning in showing more cleavage than I probably should have been and he seemed to be enjoying it. 'I've got something to tell you Sarah, and I've been putting it off for a while now but I wanted to see how things went so I feel I should tell you'. My immediate thoughts:

1. Married.
2. Gay. He wasn't sure if he was but meeting me made him realise he was. That would be just my luck.
3. He has a twitch!

'I've been offered a job in America and I'm leaving in about a month. It's with another orchestra and I'm going to be in charge of it. It's a good opportunity for me and I need to leave where I am now as I can't work with my ex any longer'.

I was gutted and kept thinking about how bad life can be sometimes. I tried to be blasé about the whole thing. He was only going for three months but that may as well be a life time when you're in a potentially new relationship. 'You can come and visit me, that would be great'.

'Oh yes that would be fantastic, I adore America'.

The evening carried on and we enjoyed a good laugh. We then walked to our cars and said the awkward goodnight thing. It was still a really lovely evening, despite the time of year, we were by the river and it was all quiet and still. Our pub is at the end of a road/cul-de-sac type thing and so there was no through traffic. The moon was out too and we could both feel the tension between us. We just knew we were going to kiss. He had lovely eyes and my God I really did want to have a bloody good snog and be engulfed in a man's arms. I've had a lovely evening Sarah. Can I kiss you?' 'I'd like that very much'.

He drew me closer, enveloped me in his arms, stared at me with his gorgeous chocolate brown eyes and smiled (thankfully no twitch at this point as I think I may have laughed). 'You're a very attractive woman Sarah'. My heart was pounding with excitement as I knew I was going to have a 'snog' for the first time in ages. He still smelt so delicious; a really masculine smell. He's taller than me too and I felt protected by his presence. He leaned in very slowly, I could feel his breath on my lips and then... Mills and Boon moment over! His tongue was shoved right down my throat without so much as a by your leave. It was like having a raw chicken fillet in there. I didn't know what to do because there wasn't much room for manoeuvre. If he'd opened his eyes he'd have seen the look of sheer panic and shock on my face and had the decency to stop.

Eventually, he came up for air. 'That was lovely Sarah, you're such a good kisser'. 'Thanks, you are too'. So he kissed me again. He'd passed that much fluid from his mouth to mine I could feel my ankles swelling with all of his spit. I nearly got lock jaw and eventually had to pull away. I can't believe I put myself through these things! My jaw is still aching from being in the same position for hours. Bloody hell Sarah you have done something really bad in a previous life to deserve such disasters.

Friday
Simon won't leave me alone. It's been such a long time since I 'dated' that I don't know if this is what happens in a relationship.

There doesn't appear to be a minute that goes by without a text from him about crap that's gone on in his day. Anyway, he met Jo-Jo today and he was actually jealous of him. He was trying to talk over Jo-Jo and the look of frustration was quite alarming. How could he be jealous of a young child?

Sunday

Okay, I think this is getting too much now. I know I joked about having photos of potential suitors on the wall of my 'dating den' and burning them if it all went wrong, but I think Simon is a bit weird. I'd not long put Jo-Jo to bed and was relaxing with a glass of red. Simon and I were talking on the phone about various things and he started telling me how his ex wife had told him how rubbish sex was with him (I have to say I was thinking that if he made love the same way he kissed, I can't say as I blame her). I sat on the sofa not knowing quite how to answer him, just thinking I don't really need/want/desire to hear this to be honest. I don't think Simon and I are going to be together for much longer. He's coming over for dinner and staying the night next Friday so we'll see how that goes.

Saturday

Well what a disaster last night was. I spent the afternoon getting myself spruced up and cooked a meal I'd never attempted before. I had a lovely bath and shaved 'The Lost Gardens of Heligan'. It's been a long time! I painted my nails and sprayed perfume in places I shouldn't have done as it stung. I was cooking a pasta dish with stilton. I knew Simon liked stilton so I was safe! He arrived with a bouquet of beautiful flowers and a bottle of wine. I'd dressed up but he looked scruffy. I finished cooking the dinner whilst he talked to me about himself. I don't think he even asked about my day at all. It was all about him. I served the pasta in a lovely big pasta dish and made it look pretty with spinach leaves and tomatoes. I'm not the greatest cook, but I was really pleased with what I'd done. I started eating it and thought it was lovely and was relieved it hadn't curdled, burnt or dried up.

Again, Simon was talking about himself and just tucked into his like we were a married couple and he'd come home 'for me tea'. I kept thinking he'd comment on it in a minute. He obviously liked it as he had second helpings. In the end I was getting rather pissed off and asked him if he liked it? Yes lovely, was his reply. So we drank the wine and I got pissed. He was still talking about himself and his sodding violin and orchestra! Eventually, he decided to try it on. Let's be honest here, women have needs as much as men and I wanted that feeling of being sexy. God it was a painful experience (not physically) but I really wished I'd not bothered. We ended up on the floor and he kept complaining about his back. So we then moved back onto the sofa and even that was wrong.

'I hurt my back a few years ago and it's not been the same since. I can't lie on the floor with you on top, it just won't work'.

Thanks for that.

'Okay, well why don't we go upstairs?' We got ourselves undressed with no seduction. Sex was just awful, thankfully there was no sign of the twitch because I think I would have just stood up, hands up in an air of resignation way, and just say look Simon, you and your bloody twitch need to get going, cos this is crap. He snored all bloody night as well. I'm used to peace and quiet and being able to lie diagonally in the bed if I wish. When we woke up in the morning, he got a bit frisky and I ended up giving him a 'Barclays Bank'. He liked this and decided to deposit his goods all over me, a little bit of which went into my eye and stung like hell. He didn't even apologise! I'm fuming even now. He's got to go before I get a nervous twitch.

Monday

I've been right about Simon all along. He is very weird. He was supposed to be coming down to spend the evening with me

Saturday night, but I just had a nagging feeling that I shouldn't go through with it. Let's be honest here, the guy's a tosser. So I took the chicken's way out and dumped him by text Friday morning. I just couldn't bear speaking to him. 'Hi Simon, really sorry but I'm not feeling very well at all, I think I've caught Jo-Jo's bug so need to cancel. I don't feel we should see each other again either, but thanks for the time we've spent and good luck in America.' I pressed 'send' and dropped the phone. God sent it now, panic. Then, I received the following text, which I will always shudder at. *'I'm in a hotel on the way back to Mum and Dad's as you've just finished with me. I've drunk the wine I bought you, watched the DVD I bought you and wanked all over the underwear I bought you'*. I gasped so loudly I nearly choked. The girls in the office wondered what the hell was wrong. I read out the text to them and they gasped just as loudly as me.

So, here we go again. I think I'm going to name my conquests. I'll be *Snow White* and they can be my dwarfs! Number one is 'Goofy' and this one can be 'Twitcher'.

Wednesday, December.

I'm beginning to wonder if people are being complete tossers just to wind me up. I've been chatting to Graham from Lancashire who is just divine. I feel safe with him, as he's not around the corner from me and so can't stalk me. Just my type, tall, funny, thick set, lovely looking thighs, from what I can see, and a gorgeous smile. We chat most nights and I gave him my mobile number a couple of days ago. Will I ever learn? A couple of hours before he phoned me he sent me a smiley face. For fuck's sake how old are you? Our conversation lasted about three minutes because he was 'watching the pennies' and couldn't spend long on the phone. What can you say to that?

Thursday

It's official. I'm retiring from Internet dating. Let's face it. I've met

Goofy and Twitcher and that all went horribly wrong and also had a brief encounter with the Lancashire Tosspot. I have taken myself off all sites and will concentrate on other things. What those things are remains to be seen but it's better than being pestered by complete tossery arseholes!

Chapter 8

When 'Hogwarts' came to Town

Sunday, March, 2006.

At last I have met Fat Bird! What can I say without sounding bitchy? Nothing, so let's just go for it. When you imagine the woman your husband is leaving you for, you picture slim, long poker straight hair, tanned, sporty and I would say no morals, but that just sounds nasty and bitter. Well, what a shock I've had today. It was about 2.00pm, Jo-Jo was with Chris and Fat Bird for the weekend and I was just settling down for a rare Sunday afternoon siesta. I treasure 'my time' weekends and I really miss Jo-Jo when he's away but as soon as he's back with his demonic attitude, it makes me question and I had a child because? How can something so young and small wind you up so quickly and to the point where you think that being locked away for a serious crime, in your own quiet cell, TV and three meals a day, seems a better option?

Shortly after adopting the siesta position on the sofa, the phone rang. I could see it was Chris; 'Hi, erm Johnathan's been sick in the car. I think it was because he woke up too quickly. He's fine, but wants you.'

What could I say to that? Bloody hell Chris, deal with it, he's your son too, but I guess he knows me better than you. After all, you naffed off with Fat Bird when the umbilical cord was still attached. I refrained from that and actually said, 'Oh bless him, bring him back. What time do you think you'll be here?'

I had about half an hour to sort myself out before they arrived. I kept looking out of the lounge window for Chris's car. I've got the 'secretly spying out the window lest he see me', down to a fine art. He's normally back at 5.00pm so I make myself at home in the dug out at 4.55pm. It's difficult in the winter because all the lights are on and I can't peek behind the curtains for an eternity. When he's back I do my timed to a fine art, Olympic sized step in a millisecond to the left and hide. It's so well practised I almost feel like doing a gymnastic finish of arms up in the air and smiling at the imaginary judges for my marks. However, I was uncertain of the time today so was out of my comfort zone and decided to put the bins out. I know how to live.

I turned as I heard a car driving the 100 yards to the top of the cul-de-sac. Life suddenly went into slow motion, and I saw my hair swishing in a big arc to catch up with me, just like those really irritating shampoo ads – and yes I know I'm worth it. There, in front of me in the driver's seat of an electric blue Ford Focus was the woman who had turned my life upside down. The very same woman who had ruined the birth of my Jo-Jo and made me feel it was all a mockery. This was the woman who was responsible for taking away 'my Chris'. Jo-Jo's life would never be conventional thanks to her. I had so many questions for her and here she was driving up to the front door of the house I had to move to because I couldn't afford to live in the needlessly extended family house I had created with Chris.

Whilst my first concern should have been for Jo-Jo, I suddenly thought shit, what the hell do I look like? I really hadn't expected to come face-to-face with her. Thank heaven for small miracles, but it was one of the rare Sundays I decided to still put on make-up. I was wearing white linen trousers and black cross over top to compliment my assets. My hair was good and I had lip gloss on!

I was about to meet a woman who had heard so much about me, one hundred per cent of it negative I expect. I was the woman who didn't love her husband, didn't understand him, got pregnant on purpose to trap him, wasn't that attractive and who was crap in bed too. So, I could play it one of two ways. Be the bitch she expected so that Chris would feel vindicated, or be the total opposite to what she would expect. Let her drive off after meeting me, worrying about how nice and attractive, I am.

Nothing would give me more pleasure than knowing she's worried sick whenever Chris and me meet up again. Before, I've just been 'the ex', the woman with no face and no substance. However, I now exist and am very much a real person. I needed to be nice.

I went straight to the back of the car and picked Jo-Jo out. He didn't smell particularly pleasant but I didn't care. He looked so happy to see me and I really played on it. I ignored Fat Bird to begin with and acted very nonchalantly. Let her sweat for a bit. She had no idea how I was going to be towards her and I liked the power. Inside I was shaking terribly, but wasn't going to show it. Chris got out of the passenger seat; the look of absolute panic on his face was priceless. I'd never seen him look so scared. Even his pupils looked dilated! Imagine the following scenarios:

Chris, you left me for a Walrus?

You left me for that? I know your eyesight's bad Chris, but my God, have you seen what's next to you?

Bloody hell Chris, she's got bigger thighs than you.

Hey, are those your trousers she's wearing?

Did you meet her playing rugby, while you were both shaving in the changing room?

But instead I resisted the devil in my head and still cradling Jo-Jo in my arms I slowly bent down and peered into the car, 'Hi, nice to put a face to the name.'

'Hi, you too' came her reply. I told Chris to take Jo-Jo's dirty clothes into the house. He was gone for about ten seconds, but it must have felt like a lifetime to him. I would love to know what was going through his mind! Fat Bird had one hand on the gear stick. I say *hand*; it was more like a podgy lump of lard with sausages on the end. I noticed something dull on her ring finger. It looked like it was just a diamond on there, but I'm sure there must have been a band of gold hanging on for dear life in there somewhere. I know, I know, I sound really nasty, however, and this is a big however, Chris is extremely materialistic. He lived a champagne lifestyle on lemonade money – lemonade money we didn't have so it all went on credit. He was very flash. So, when I spotted this excuse of a solitaire diamond on her ring finger, I inwardly gasped. Fat Bird had her greasy black hair scraped back to a ponytail, almost giving her a bad face-lift. Not a scrap of make-up on, jeans and a black t-shirt top with small straps.

I looked at Chris in amazement who, incidentally, was turning grey – was he really holding his breath? His ex-wife and third wife to be were engaging in conversation. I could have had a field day and ranted and raved at Fat Bird, but I didn't. I really had to fight to keep the voices in my head from escaping through my mouth to say, what does it feel like to be responsible for a child growing up without his Dad living with him? You do realise you'll be wife number three. And just for the record, I loved Chris very much. If there were problems in our marriage he certainly didn't let me know. Trust me; there are certainly two sides to every story. So watch him like a hawk. I never guessed he was having an affair, but he's obviously a great liar. You're obviously desperate to be with someone no matter what and I wish you both the happiness you deserve.

A good day!

Sunday, April.
Jo-Jo is picking up on things now and his ears prick up when I say the name 'Chris'. So based upon my now brilliant visual imagery of Mary and Chris they shall both now be known Hagrid (Mary) and Voldermort (Chris). Honestly, I'm not being nasty, the likeness to Hagrid is uncanny, she's just not quite as tall as him, and obviously has had her beard lasered!

Weird Wednesday
Here we go again. For weeks now I've been feeling irritable. Not run of the mill PMT irritable, this is much worse. I feel tired, and my stomach is doubled up in knots. I have headaches and just

don't have enthusiasm for anything. This has gone on too long now and I think I'm going to see my doctor. I'm still doing my relaxing exercise regime before I go to bed, which is helping, but this is something deeper and I don't feel right.

Tuesday (Me and my new friend – Prozac.)
That's it, life as I know it is now over. I'm officially going mad. Not only do I have to send my son off to Hagrid and Voldermort every other weekend, but the time has now come for me to resort to potions and the 'dark arts' to fix my moody mind too. My doctor has diagnosed 'mild depression'. That word 'depression' is going to be hard to get used to. When I hear it I think of mad people sitting in straight jackets, rocking back and forth. I'm not depressed. I had a lovely weekend, saw friends, had a laugh. I wouldn't be laughing if I was depressed would I?

The rest of the consultation was a blur. I felt I should wait in the pharmacy, not just for my prescription, but also for the tattoo artist to tattoo 'leper' or a pentagram on my forehead to ward people off. As I was waiting, I wondered if all the pharmacists were judging me. Mind you, on the flip side, if it makes me feel better and able to cope with a three year old who's developing the mind of a stubborn eighty year old, then bring it on! I phoned Mum when I got home and announced that her youngest daughter is now reliant on anti-depressants.

I've been so preoccupied in bringing Jo-Jo up, moving home, working etc that it's all come to a head. I do get stressed and seem to become irritable very quickly. I know I'm not a natural Mum and do resent Chris for just upping sticks without any consideration for Jo-Jo or me. I don't get any time for myself and life has got on top of me just recently, so maybe these will help. I've had the first one, so watch this space.

Thursday, June. (Two months with my new best friend!)
I'm in love! Not for real unfortunately, but with my new 'bestest'

friend Prozac. I did some research on depression and now actually feel bloody proud of getting this far. Research states that I should have been treated for Post Traumatic Stress Disorder, after Jo-Jo's birth.

When I think about it, I was just left to get on with it. I thought that PTSD was something people in the Armed Forces had when they came back from a war zone, not people like me. Although, having said that, after a day with Jo-Jo playing with a friend, my lounge can sometimes resemble a war zone. I have also decided that I will not allow myself to feel that there's a stigma attached to being on Prozac. I have a child to bring up and that in itself brings a trailer load of challenges so I have come to the conclusion that Prozac is my substitute husband! If I had a proper, bona fide husband then he would take away some of the stress and we would work as a team. This is exactly what 'Pro' and I do now. I do the physical stuff and he relaxes me and ratio-nalises my thoughts for me. Job done! I still feel tired and irritable sometimes, that's life, but I've noticed that my anxiety has reduced dramatically and I'm able to tell myself to not be so bloody stupid if I start having silly unrealistic thoughts. I hope that Pro and I have a very long and happy relationship together.

September
Yesterday was a very weird day for me. I know that Voldermort got married to Hagrid at the weekend in Florida. I suppose he's exhausted all the English venues. Not that I'd ever want him back, but it's still strange to know that he's got married again and there's another Mrs Chilton out there.

Friday, October.
Have discovered Ebay! What a truly great site for poor people like me. I would love to be able to go to my favourite shops and have a spending spree and not even think about what I've spent, just for once in my life. I love clothes and would have so many if

I could afford it. I've just won a top from M&S for less than the price of a bottle of cheap wine. Amazing! No one needs to know. I'm adapting to this life very well I think.

February, 2007.
Had a call from Chris's godmother, Eleanor today. Hagrid has had a miscarriage and is depressed. She's apparently not sure if she wants to be with Chris now and needs to sort out her life. The first bit is sad, I wouldn't wish that on anyone, but I do have to laugh at Chris potentially thinking shit, where will I go if she finishes with me? Apparently Hagrid nearly called off the engagement because she found something disagreeable on Chris's computer. I am concluding it could be one or all of the following:

1. Pornography
2. Chat rooms
3. Internet dating sites
4. Teach yourself 'Morris Dancing'.

I personally would be more worried about point number 4. Still, it's given me some satisfaction knowing that all is not well in 'Hogwarts'.

Sunday, March.
Could life get any worse? I was going shopping with Mum yesterday for the day to Exeter and really looking forward to it. I'd saved up some money to take us both out to lunch to celebrate Mother's Day weekend. Typically, the post arrived early that morning and I took it upstairs to open whilst I got ready. I only had one envelope. It was brown with 'Children's Services' stamped in big capital letters on the front. I automatically thought it was something to do with Jo-Jo starting school in September. But it wasn't that at all. It makes me feel sick writing

it down. The letter actually read...

Dear Mrs Chilton

I am writing to inform you that Children's Services have received an anonymous referral via the NSPCC in relation to your care of Johnathan. The anonymous referral was received via the NSPCC from an adult who has good knowledge of the family. Allegations centre around areas of emotional well-being and referrer specifies the following:

1. *That Mum shouts, swears and hits Johnathan, 'constantly rejecting him'.*
2. *That Mum has depression and has had it for years.*
3. *That Mum shows no warmth and has never 'bonded' with Johnathan.*
4. *That Johnathan is quite aggressive and hits other children.*

I was to go and see them on Thursday. Thursday? I want to sort this out now. I could have been sick. How could anyone be so cruel? I'm not allowed to find out because it's anonymous. Why would someone say such nasty things? Everyone close to me knows how hard I've found life over the last couple of years. I've not always had patience with Jo-Jo, but I bloody love him and would die for him. Whoever you are, you're a bitch.

Apparently it was a female caller, who said I never kiss and cuddle Jo-Jo. Why me? What have I done? I'm not going to get over this for a very long time and will constantly be looking over my shoulder to see who's watching me. I've done nothing wrong and sometimes feel like the worst Mum in world as it is, so I don't need some obviously vindictive bitch to do this to me.

Monday

Saw the manager at Children's Services today. He was a very nice man who put me at ease. I was on the phone to them first thing to sort this letter out. I've not slept all weekend and it's knocked me sideways. I took Jo-Jo with me as I wanted the manager to see him and how he interacted with people. He was happy after talking to me and said that I wouldn't believe the amount of anonymous calls they get from vindictive spouses, estranged families etc. Whilst it made me feel slightly better, it's still 'out there'. Whoever you are, I hope you got a kick out of this. Your life is probably shit and you saw me coping so you thought you'd try and drag me down to your level. Today it's worked, but tomorrow I'll dust myself off and carry on.

Wednesday, July.

I don't believe it; the NSPCC thing has come to rear its head again. Whilst I'll never forget what happened, it was sort of fading into the background . However, I had a home visit from Jo-Jo's new teacher today and so told her about the call. I have nothing to hide but I felt ashamed telling her. She was lovely and didn't comment really but I wanted them to know what some sad cow has done.

Tuesday, August.

I obviously didn't give the proper reaction the first time. The bitch has done it again. I've had another call to the NSPCC. This time, though, Children's Services have phoned Jo-Jo's nursery and had a chat with them, plus my doctor and actually closed the case. It's really not fair that I can't find out who it was. I shall be on egg shells waiting for another one. I've done nothing wrong. All I'm doing is trying to be the best parent I can under what have been very hard circumstances.

Sloppy Sunday (Steve Wright Love Songs)

Is it me or has this show changed? I used to enjoy listening to Steve Wright Sunday Love Songs when Chris first left. Just because I was married to a two timing bastard, doesn't mean I wouldn't wish happiness on anyone else. In the early days Mum was invariably with me on a Sunday as she would come for the weekend and give me a mental and physical break from motherhood and we would have it on in the background when Jo-Jo was having his morning nap and I was cleaning my unnecessarily extended house. Mum and I would listen to the dedications. Hello Steve, my name is Adam and I'd like to dedicate a song to my lovely wife, Anna. We've been married for 40 years on Tuesday and I love her more now than when we first met. Thank you Anna for two wonderful children and five gorgeous grandchildren. I can't wait to spend the next 40 years with you. You are my world.

Mum would pretend to gag whilst I would be getting all emotional and thinking how sweet. I want to love again and this programme makes me think that I could have it. In a way I think the programme gave me hope and I would religiously listen to it. Several years on, a few dwarfs the wiser and a life on my own, pleasing myself, it's a completely different story. I'm now the one gagging when I hear the dedications. Today was an impatient eye roller and one where you couldn't help but shout at the woman for being so stupid. Hello Steve, Karen here from North Yorkshire. Please could you play a romantic record for my partner, Justin? We've been together for six months and it's been the best six months of my life. Between us we have six gorgeous children and I love him more than anything in this world. He's 300 miles away working hard and I miss him terribly. Thanks Steve.

My immediate comment to this was Oh for God's sake woman get a grip. He's 300 miles away, only been with you for six months, he's probably shagging his heart out. Wake up and smell the used condom. I would never say I'm anti men, that will never happen, but I don't believe that there is one man for each of us. I used to. I think there are many people out there who we'll get on with, but it's how we deal with the temptation that counts. We could all fall for someone who's married and think they're the 'one' and it's just not working out with their wife/husband. In some cases, that is true, but it's how you get together that counts.

Since being on my own, I've met men with whom I could have had either a fling or relationship. One thing I've observed is that you become a target of married men's attention when you're single, especially if you're a single Mum. Whilst it's really nice to get the attention from a man, it's more tempting to say to them, 'Look, I maybe single sweetheart, but I don't *need* attention, especially from you. You obviously crave it but I'm stronger than that and can actually cope on my own, now naff off.'

Wednesday, September.
Jo-Jo starts school tomorrow. I can't believe this day has arrived. He's one month away from being four and a half, yet it doesn't seem more than a nappy change since he was born. I've obviously had wine this evening and have got upset because this is one of many major events that will happen in Jo-Jo's life that should have been shared by Chris and I together. No sir, I did not sign up for this. When you find out you're pregnant, you enter the world of daydreaming about baby's first words, first crawl, first steps, first tooth. You then move on to first day at school and mentally imagine them grown up and married before they've even left the womb!

So, when I was spending time allowing myself to daydream about what life would be like with my new baby and talked to Chris about first days at school, if anyone had told me I would be on my own with Jo-Jo when he was still so very young I would have looked at them as if they'd actually told me my husband was born a girl and had had a promising career as a prima ballerina.

Chris was my life and we had decided, consciously, to start a family. I think I need to stop drinking, as I'm getting a bit morbid. My little baby's starting school. I've worked so hard since he was crawling to mould his character. From a very young age you teach your child good manners, how to share, how to play nicely with other children, how to eat politely, knowing that in a few years time they would be starting school and putting into practise what you'd taught them. This is the time the umbilical cord is well and truly severed. Pre school, you choose who your child plays with, you find a nice circle of Mums, go to baby/toddler groups of your choosing and just hope and pray that your child doesn't zone in to the child that all parents look at with pure hatred.

Thursday (very early in the morning.)
'Muuuummmmmeeeeeee, I'm starting school today, wake up!' Who needs an alarm clock when you have a child? I just need five minutes to savour this moment. I'm feeling nervous, excited, sad, all at once. He looks so smart in his grey trousers, white shirt, green and red tie and bottle green jumper, finished off with black leather school shoes. They cost more than what I budget for a week's worth of food. His feet are a size thirteen, so not overly big, yet I couldn't believe the price. I asked if there was a free clock radio with them. Anyway, I took the obligatory photograph of Jo-Jo and me all dressed smartly in his new school uniform and empty book bag which he insisted on holding. This photo will be around for a long time to come and I need to ensure that my hair looks good and I'm not showing all of my chins in one go.

Jo-Jo was so looking forward to starting school and had really out grown nursery. He was getting bored there and looked so grown up compared to the other children. Being so tall for his age, he looked like he was on work experience from the local junior school, but he was only four! He was having problems with his tie and it's been a few years since I've had to tie one. First attempt not good, but it's nice to know that if I needed to, I could tie a reef knot.

7.50am leave house to pick up Jo-Jo's friend, Joseph. Both boys just unbearably excited. Walked to school with Sue, Joseph's Mum, both of us feeling anxious by this time. 8.30am arrive at school. School whistle goes at 8.50am but, typical me, I'm early again. Jo-Jo and Joseph are running around the playground like deer trying to frantically escape a pride of lions. Why do all the other children seem to be calm and standing in line? I'm looking around me trying to suss out all the other parents, and thankfully they look okay.

8.50am whistle blows and the children stand in line. Sue and I are trying desperately to fight back tears and feel all eyes on us and I just want the ground to open up in front of me. We all take our children in, fight back tears, give them a kiss and an enormous hug, and wave at them. They look at us as if they're about to be evacuated and going to board a train to some spooky boarding school in a faraway land (images of the Harry Potter films appear before me). We then smile and keep waving and are told by the teacher that they will stop crying soon (once she turns them all into frogs I seem to hear her say). Thanks for that, that's going to make my day run really well. I went back to Sue's for a cuppa and a nostalgia trip. I know I didn't enjoy the first few years of parenthood and wished Jo-Jo to grow up, but my God I really couldn't believe this day was here. Chris didn't even ring to wish Jo-Jo well for his first day at school. I'm so cross with him.

Sue and I walked down to school to pick up the boys and they came bounding down the steps with a painted picture. It was still slightly wet due to the fact that they'd probably used two litres of paint on an A4 sheet. It was very, shall we say, modern art. I need to learn how to lie very well over the next few years at school. 'Oh that's lovely Jo-Jo, really well painted. I'm not good at guessing so you tell me what it is'. Do you remember those pictures to test your eyesight? If you look hard enough you can see a number. Children's pictures are a bit like that in my opinion. What appeared to be blobs of red, blue, yellow, green and black paint literally poured onto the paper, was obviously a rocket, if you looked really closely and used your wildest imagination. So, first day over, and I have a very tired child on my hands. I put Jo-Jo to bed early. I collapsed on the sofa, with a glass of red by my side. It's been quite a difficult day and one that deserves some medicinal comfort. I'm crying again, mainly relief that the first day is over. However, this is yet something else I've got to learn to tackle on my own. Cheers Chris you sod. I owe you, big time.

October

I'm getting good at this at this self-counselling stuff. Pad has disappeared. Now I physically push to one side stupid stuff that comes into my head. I've taught myself to stop analysing every-thing and carry on with my lovely dream – it doesn't involve children and it's all about me. I'm feeling more rested too as a result, which is making me feel more with it.

Wednesday, November.

Winter is looming and every bloody evening's the same. We come home, Jo-Jo gets tired and arsey, I cook dinner, he moans about what it is, we learn his key words, he has a bath whilst I'm running around like a blue arse fly upstairs tidying up, we read a book together, he goes to sleep at 7.30pm. I then sit in the lounge watching crap on the television, or channel hop, watching tumbleweed float through the lounge. It's going to be a long winter. It's no good, I need to do something to make the evenings pass and stimulate me (and I really can't go back to the whole Internet dating debacle). I Googled home study counselling courses and found one at a good university and decide to take Jayne's offer up to lend me the money to pay for it. By the end of the course, I will have a Diploma in Counselling. Having looked at the course content, I've been through half of what I'll be learning about so, if nothing else, it'll be cathartic.

Monday

I have researched the 'web' extensively and also learning lots from my new course and I think I may have a bit of anxiety. What I'm doing is worrying about simple stuff i.e. did I speak to my friend nicely today? Have I upset her? That then leads on to me thinking that I probably have and how can I make it up to her. Should I text? What if she doesn't reply? It's all very stupid but, quite frankly, it's taking over my life. What I've taught myself to do is to write down my worry, analyse and rationalise it.

I'm going to demonstrate this for you darling diary so that I can refer back to it when I have another episode of paranoia and have forgotten what to do!

Incident – At play centre today with Louise. All going fine but I didn't think she said goodbye nicely and now I'm worried I've upset her.

My feelings – I left there feeling; worried, pissed off, annoyed at myself for thinking this, and quite deflated.

How am I feeling (on a scale of 1-100) 45 per cent

Most poignant thought – Worried

Analyse poignant thought – We had a lovely time at the play centre but her daughter, Rebecca, was being a pain and not sitting down properly and was throwing food, so she was probably fed up and had had enough. I've known Louise for years so she obviously feels she doesn't have to put on any airs and graces with me. I think I'm the only friend she can do this with.

My feelings now – Relief, reassured, annoyed with myself.

How am I feeling (on a scale of 1-100) 65 per cent

Look I've improved by 20 per cent just by writing down how I feel. I've printed out blank sheets to take with me everywhere I go, just in case. I'm good at this; I think I ought to do it for a living! My course is going well and I'm thoroughly enjoying it. When Jo-Jo was first born, at about two weeks old, I can remember saying that I was going to help women who had been through the ordeal I went through. Perhaps now is the right time. Okay, I'm on Prozac and still get anxiety, but I'm treating it myself and if I can do that, who's to say I can't pass on my knowledge and experience to others? Ooh, I'm getting a bit excited now. I really do need a mental challenge and something that will allow my experiences to help others, even if only to show them what not to do!

February, 2008. (Hagrid and Voldermort have done the deed)
Chris phoned me last evening. 'I just wanted to phone you to let you know that Mary is pregnant.

'Oh good'. Now, I said this in a right, now you'll know exactly what it's like being a proper parent and not one who picks and chooses when they want to be one, kind of way.

'Thanks Sarah, I'm glad you've taken it so well. Baby's due in December. I'll tell Johnathan when I see him at the weekend but I didn't want you to hear it from him'.

'No problem, thanks for letting me know'. I'm biting my tongue so hard that I nearly pierce it. He really thinks I'm pleased for them both. I personally think it's hilarious. He abandoned his first son and thought he was father of the year. He can't abandon this one too. His 'friends' bought his last story that we apparently hadn't been getting on for a long time and decided to have a child to help the relationship. I was livid when I heard that. Anyway, he can't do this again as that excuse is old news. I phoned Mum straightaway and both of us couldn't stop laughing at the sleepless nights he'll have and can't run away from. I went to sleep knowing that justice is doing his job!

Thursday, December.
Chris phoned earlier on to say that Mary had had a baby boy and they've named him Joshua. Would I tell Johnathan for him in the morning? I don't know how I feel really. Oh yes I do, but it's

probably not very nice. I hope he's a healthy baby, but a touch of colic, and weeks of projectile vomit and no sleep would make me feel good. I was very good Di and wished him congratulations and said, 'This is where the fun starts'. Again, he thought I was being nice. He really is a bit stupid!

Saturday, April, 2008.
I'm really hoping that this will be the last year of manic, stressful, chaotic, noisy and, inevitably, at some point, tearful, parties. I've had my fill of fun houses to be quite frank. I know they're for the children, but I fail to see the fun in any of it. I've been to quieter nightclubs and football matches. Children are just so loud. If I ever owned a children's play centre (would rather snog a rotting corpse) I would hand out ear plugs to the grown ups and take sadistic pleasure in blowing a whistle really loudly and shouting for God's sake shut up and keep the noise down! There are parents here trying to talk and drink coffee in peace. The next person who screams, laughs, shouts, cries, or shows any sign of enjoyment, will sit on the step outside for ten minutes. Now play quietly.

Anyway, Jo-Jo's fifth birthday party tomorrow is at bloody Laser World. Not only do I have the privilege of paying for it, I have to actually join in. A few weeks ago I told Jo-Jo that he could have nine friends, plus him, which would make the numbers even for fighting. The look on his face was both distress and shock and then said, 'But Mummy you're playing too'. I was sipping my usual evening glass of wine at this time. I say evening, it had been a stressful day at work today, so I decided to move my 'Wine Watershed' back to 5.00pm. Thankfully I had chosen a white wine for this evening's company, as I sort of sprayed it out over the sofa in shock.

'Me? I'm playing?' I asked in a panic stricken voice, as I ran for some kitchen roll to mop up my tsunami.

'Oh please Mummy, I want you to'. I could tell he was going

to start crying, so I put on my of course I'm going to do it, I was only teasing look. 'Good. I'd like Dad to come too'. At that point the whole bottle came out of the fridge. If Hagrid comes too then I shall ask for real lasers!

Saturday (B-day)

Jo-Jo was so excited, he was almost demonic! He was watching the clock wishing every second away until he could meet his friends at Laser World. There was much excitement in the over crowded waiting area. Ten five and six year olds running around like headless chickens waiting to go in and become 'Storm Troopers'. Chris strutted in. We could just about manage to say hello to each other. I got quite excited because he asked me if I'd paid for the party yet. I was hoping he was going to give me something towards it because it had cost me a fortune, but when it came to paying at the end he didn't offer me anything. I was so disappointed because I could have done with the money and stupidly spent most of the party thinking that he was going to contribute and almost relaxed a bit. What an arse (him, obviously).

Jo-Jo was excited to see his Dad and we all made our way down to 'base camp'. I really, really, didn't want to do this. It was my idea of hell on earth to be honest. Running around a dark room, music blasting out, wearing a backpack previously worn by sweaty snotty nosed children, shooting lasers at people. I needed alcohol. Thankfully Sue came with me for support. 'Don't worry Sarah, it'll all be over soon. You can be Luke Skywalker and I'll be Obi-Wan Kenobi!' 'Okay that's a good idea and Chris will be Chewbacca'. Jo-Jo was glued to his Dad and seemed to parade him around like a trophy. Chris had never been to any of his parties before and I think Jo-Jo was enjoying this moment. I used to feel like that. I was so proud to be on Chris's arm, showing off this tall, broad, dark and handsome man. Now, I'd rather boil my own head in someone else's vomit.

We all kitted up, were read the riot act by the unenthusiastic 'boy' who was leading us and then we were off. I smiled, but inside I was dying and still trying to hydrate from the wine I'd consumed the night before to blot out what lay ahead of me today. I did the sign of the cross on my chest and reticently strolled into hell on earth with Sue. The floor was black, as were the walls with an excuse for a solar system painted at one end. Everywhere were black pillars and mini mazes for the little storm troopers to run through and hide. It was pretty impressive I have to say, but I spotted a seat and every so often Sue and I sat down and cheered on the children.

However, and this is a big however, every bloody laser you fire gets recorded and every sodding laser that hits your backpack gets recorded. Sue and I suddenly got competitive. There I was taking great joy in shooting endless lasers at unsuspecting six year olds when suddenly, Chris started appearing everywhere I went. I was taking cover behind a pillar whilst guarding our base camp and you should have seen the way I was holding the gun, it was so Luke Skywalker. I peered round and there was Chris, standing there as cool as a cucumber shooting lasers directly at me. I'm sure he thought he was still in the bloody TA. Stupid arse.

God damn it this was war; there was no time to have fun. I crossed my chest again at reaching my next vantage point and there he was again shooting at me. He was distracted by someone shooting at him and I ran to the other side of the room, which again was very SAS like as I wanted to win now. I lost Sue as she was also in her old Star Wars world. I was looking around for kids to shoot and this head appeared from behind a pillar and started shooting at me . It was Chris again and all I could think was bloody hell how did he get there? Why me? Why me? He was aiming for my head as well! The whistle went and we all stopped for a break. I didn't give Chris the satisfaction of knowing that he was annoying me and just laughed with the children. 'Sue, I need

your back this time, Chewbacca is after me and we need to win'.
'Yes Master Sky Walker'.

Chris was looking quite serious at this stage and was ready to
go again. Mind you, so were me and Sue. Jogging on the spot,
limbering up our necks and shoulders and trying to give our
team some instructions on how to win. They appeared to understand what was said to them, but did they do as they were told
when the lights went off? Did they heck. I immediately ran and
hid. There was a raised area in the room and no one seemed to
be going there as it was quite out of the way. This was war! Stone
me he just seemed to morph from behind a pillar and shoot me
in the head at practically point blank range. The name
Voldermort really suits him, as he seems to have developed an
ability to just appear at any given time.

I tried to enjoy myself for the rest of the game but everywhere
I looked Voldermort was there shooting at me. I half expected
him to shout 'Expeliarmus' and point his gun at me by this time.
Full time whistle went and I was desperate to find out how our
team had done. I wanted to beat Chris's team, but it was Jo-Jo's
party and I knew there would be tears if his team had lost. Jo-Jo's
face was a picture because his team did actually win. He was
jumping up and down with excitement and laughing. Chris's
face was also a picture. He had a smug look on his face and I'm
sure he was fighting back the urge to punch the air and join in
with the kids. Silly man.

Then came the food. Ten sweaty, smelly and fired up children
to try and calm down. Chris actually joined in and helped with
the food and drink. For a split second I imagined how my life
could have been. The two of us still married and celebrating our
son's fifth birthday. It's how I wanted it to be... and I'm back in
the room again. Back to screaming, smelly kids getting over
excited and thinking it's hilarious to squirt too much tomato
ketchup on their plates, and on each other. The main thing for me
was that Jo-Jo was enjoying himself. He was laughing with his

friends and just enjoying being the centre of attention. Chris and I didn't speak much during the food. I took some photos of the children and just tried to keep myself busy. When it was time for the birthday cake, Chris stood back and I held the cake and sang Happy Birthday. I could feel myself welling up a bit, don't know why really as I should be used to this by now. Jo-Jo blew out the candles and the cake was taken away to be cut up for the party bags.

Chris was ready to go and Jo-Jo was going to spend the night with him. 'Why don't you come back to my house and watch Jo-Jo open his presents as I need to make a note of who's bought what. 'We've got things planned at our house.' I heaved a really big sigh and fought back the tears and put on my best smile. 'Oh well, not to worry. You go and have a great time Jo-Jo and remember what your friends have bought you, you'll need to write your thank you letters next week.' 'Thanks Mum, I had a great party, it was the best. Love you.' And with that he said goodbye to his friends, thanked them for coming and within seconds he was a blot on the landscape walking out with Chris who was carrying the presents.

In my head I'm shouting, 'That's right Chris, you just walk away with our son and enjoy the glory. Don't worry I'll settle the bill for this party, and the next one, and the one after that probably. I'll ensure all the thank you notes are written and deal with the crap I'll get when he doesn't want to do them. Honestly, it's no problem, you just fuck off to Hagrid and enjoy the special, fun times'.

I phoned Mum when I got home and the flood gates collapsed and the tsunami appeared. 'Chin up love, trust me, you'll reap the rewards in years to come. You're a strong woman and Chris will realise just what hard work it is when his son is older and he's demanding parties, hobbies etc.' 'Thanks Mum, I appreciate that. It's just been a long, tiring and expensive afternoon'. I have mixed emotions. Relief the party is over, tiredness from making sure everyone was enjoying themselves and feeling upset because it shouldn't have been like this.

Wonderful Wednesday

I'm a counsellor Di! I've qualified. I am officially Sarah Chilton MASC Dip Couns. Get me! This is what my tutor wrote about me. *You have maintained an excellent standard throughout your course. Good luck for your future as a counsellor.* I feel so inspired now. The world is my oyster, or at least that's how it feels right now. Jo-Jo's away with Chris this weekend so I'm going to spend the whole weekend writing to midwives, hospitals, GP surgeries and Children's Centres telling them that I want to visit women who have just given birth and help them to de brief and talk about what's happened, both positive and negative. I'm going to make a difference somehow. What happened in my life was for a reason.

January, 2009 (Meeting Ron Weasley)

I said to Chris that I'll take Jo-Jo up to him, because I've asked if he'll have him an extra night which is why I've volunteered to take him. Plus I want to see the house and have a 'nosey'. I was slightly nervous as meetings are normally on my territory and I have the upper hand, but as we turned up in the cul-de-sac, butterflies started fluttering in my tummy. Chris opened the door and Jo-Jo walked straight in to the lounge. I needed the loo so used the downstairs one. Hagrid has quite nice taste actually, nice white suite with turquoise accessories. I personally wouldn't have put the ironing board in there but I suppose there's nowhere else to put it. I walked into the lounge, eyes working overtime trying to suss out as much as I could about my surroundings, kicking myself that I hadn't put a hidden camera in my coat button.

I noticed a rather large TV, typical Chris, and also the 'art' on the wall. He could have saved himself some money and asked the local school children to have done the same thing. But then I spotted something absolutely priceless and clicked as to why Chris was looking a tad embarrassed. There, on the floor playing with his toys was Ron Weasley! Now, I've nothing at all against ginger hair. Why would I? I'm of that ilk, but Chris's brother suddenly found it funny to say things like 'gingwar' or 'ginge' to me a few years ago. Chris would laugh with him and I used to get upset at the fact that he never stood up for me. They'd laugh if they saw a ginger baby. So, you can imagine my delight and amusement that Voldermort and Hagrid had given birth to Ron Weasley! 'Hello little one. My, my what a lot of ginger hair you have. Where did you get that from? The milkman?' Sorry, couldn't resist the last bit. I think I needed some payback for all the years of torment I got from Chris's brother. Chris still looked embarrassed and I drove back home with a big smile on my face knowing that there is a God!

Chapter 9

Snow White and the Seven Dwarfs Part II

(Still optimistic? Then read on...)

Monday

Spurred on by my recent assurance that God does indeed exist and works in mysterious ways, I have decided to throw my hat back into the ring. And my plan to meet someone naturally may have paid off. My boss and I had a meeting today with a guy called Nick. He was coming in to talk to us about data storage. All rather boring but luckily Nick was gorgeous and was pure entertainment. Lovely big, muscular thighs. I had no idea at all what he was talking about as I was studying him far too hard. He was sitting in our boardroom when I arrived and gave me a really flirty smile. 'Ding Dong' Nick, welcome into my world I'm thinking. Nice firm handshake, not bad sized hands and big feet, you know what they say about the size of a man's feet – big shoes! (And a good night to be had by all!) We sat down and Nick started his sales pitch on why we should use him for data storage. At one point he actually got up to show my boss and I something on the plasma screen. His arse was just to die for. Fabulously bottom hugging jeans and thighs an England rugby player would kill for.

Well, that was it, I was a gonna. I had no idea if he was good at what he did or not, he'd got the job as far as I was concerned on his 'assets' alone! The meeting lasted approximately one hour and my boss said his obligatory 'thanks' to Nick and left it to me to wrap up the meeting. Oh, how I thought of a nice way to end the meeting, but I don't think the boardroom table would have taken the strain. Nick left and I went back to my office with a fixed grin on my face. Could this be it? He's just my type. Oh please let Cupid shoot his arrow for me, this time without missing.

Wednesday

Had about ten emails from Nick today asking me all about myself. I really must do some work tomorrow. He's got a great sense of humour. I just wish he'd ask me out.

Thursday (one week later)

Finally, after what seems like years, Nick has asked me out for a coffee. As soon as the email came in, I put up my hands like Eva Peron and shouted, 'Finally!' He's meeting me tomorrow and I'm dreading it and excited both at the same time.

Friday

I'm in love. I only had an hour so suggested Nick pick me up with a flask and we sit by the river. He arrived in a brand new Range Rover. I needed oxygen when I got in, as it was so high off the ground. We drove a short way to the river and Nick poured me a coffee and we got talking. 'So how long have you been single Nick?' 'I've been separated for a couple of years and I have to say that I'm enjoying my freedom. I do have a girlfriend but it's a very casual arrangement as I don't like to be tied down'. (You've obviously never tried it Nick!) I tried not to show disappointment on my face but why am I not meeting the right person? Why do I always see someone I like to then find out they're sodding married, engaged, or living with someone? He has a couple of children, who are fourteen and sixteen and quite self-sufficient. He does Karate in his spare time and I could just imagine him strutting his stuff. Oh I love a powerfully strong man. Sod the girlfriend, I feel like being naughty! 'After twenty years of being with Scarlett I just want some 'me' time and enjoy doing my own thing.' I can understand that but am still pissed off with the fact that he has a blasted girlfriend. I feel a bit deflated now but will see what happens. I'm just so bored and need some fun and male attention.

Wednesday (Where's Willy?)
I'm doomed and Cupid hates me. I had the day off work and kept Jo-Jo at nursery. Nick said he'd help me find a laptop as he's into computers and they bore me rigid. He picked me up in the Range Rover and I had to restrain myself from doing a royal wave on the way to Comet. It didn't take long to pick one for me and Nick came back for a coffee. We sat and talked for a while and I was doing everything I could to not be spotted copping a look at his edible thighs. As he was going he leant in and we somehow ended up kissing. It felt lovely. He slowly cupped my face in his hands in a really gentle and romantic way. I've never had anyone cup my face into their hands before and kiss me so tenderly. It was just gorgeous. I have realised recently that because I was 'abandoned' by the one person I loved so very much, it's important to feel wanted again and you grab onto any opportunity you can.

We kissed for ages. I was really enjoying myself, got a bit carried away and decided to 'cop a feel' which is where it all went horribly wrong. 'Oh Sarah, stop before things get too heated, let's not rush anything'. Too heated? There's nothing to get too heated with, where is it? Did he forget to screw it on today? Honestly, there was nothing there. I've never experienced that before. Admittedly, I was spoilt with Chris. I wanted a proper look because I just couldn't get over the fact that I couldn't feel anything at all. Not even a slight lump. His face was telling me that he was enjoying himself but my face must have been utter shock and confusion. How could someone be enjoying something that someone else is doing to them when that person can't even find the thing they're supposed to be doing something with? 'I really ought to go Sarah, but believe me I'd love to stay, that was gorgeous and you're a very sexy woman'. 'Thank you,

you are too' I didn't have the heart to ask him 'Where's Willy?' With that, he left. I'm still puzzled quite frankly at how I couldn't feel anything at all. Nothing. Zilch. I need another go.

Sunday (two weeks after 'fondle shock'.)
Really cross with Nick. He came over last night for a takeaway that I said I'd treat him to as he's set up my laptop for me and it's all working brilliantly. Bearing in mind he has his own business, no mortgage and a £60k Range Rover, he turned up with not so much as a bottle of wine. We went for a walk and then I ordered the takeaway. I'd bought two bottles of his favourite wine, which was nearly half my weekly food budget, plus the cost of the takeaway.

We sat out in the garden as it was a lovely evening, but through the whole thing I just kept thinking he was with me under duress and duty. I didn't really feel he was relaxed. After a couple of hours eating dinner, drinking and chatting I realised I was a bit tipsy and we ended up kissing. 'Why don't we take this upstairs?' suggested Nick in a provocative way. By this point we were pretty much undressed anyway. I decided to explore to see if he'd remembered to bring his tackle with him. Well, he had, but it had obviously shrunk in the wash. What was also puzzling me was the fact that it didn't seem to have the ability to stay hard. It was like a soggy sausage.

I had two options. Laugh, which was so very tempting, or just do my best Meg Ryan impression and fake it. I chose option two. Half an hour later I was getting very bored and started to sort out what Jo-Jo and I were going to have for dinner next week and what I should buy Jayne for her birthday (in two months time). If he'd gone on much longer I think I could have done a word search. He eventually finished and promptly fell asleep and snored like a pig. I elbowed him so hard that he woke up. 'Sorry Sarah, can't you sleep? Look, it's 2.00am and I've got to get up at 5.00am to pick up my brother and his wife from Bristol Airport so

I'll go'. 'You don't have to go Nick, I've bought some nice food for breakfast.' 'No, don't worry, you get some sleep'. I couldn't sleep then because I was fuming. I had just been used for a free meal and a shag. When he went all he said was 'See ya'. Nothing else, just 'See ya'. He may as well have left money on the bedside cabinet for me. Bastard.

Tuesday, August.
Nick texted me today to say hi, but I've ignored him. Cupid, whatever it is I've done, please tell me so that I can apologise. Why can I not find a man? I now have another dwarf to add to my list. Goofy, Twitcher, Tosspot and now Dickless. Well done Sarah, you sure know how to pick the good ones!

Thursday
Don't shout at me Di, I've now resorted to Internet dating, again. Bear with me and support me through what is bound to be a bumpy ride (well I can live in hope!).

Monday
Right, I'm going to actually find a decent man. Even though I wasn't 'chucked' at the altar and defrauded by a man (mind you, Dickless did by the sheer fact he lived up to his name) I'm determined not to turn into Miss Havisham and pine for the rest of my life and sit in my house gathering dust wearing my wedding dress and one shoe.

Thursday (two weeks into hunt4aman.co.uk)
It's not going well. I feel the dust building around me in true Great Expectations style. I have been propositioned by a man old enough to be my Dad and scary enough to go on *Crime Watch*.

Saturday
Right, don't want to get too excited, but I've discovered Gareth.

Lovely photo. It transpires it was taken on his last day of being in the Marines. He had me at the mere mention of the word Marines. He now works for the MOD and we've chatted for two hours on MSN tonight and I like the sound of him. Watch this space...

Monday (one week since I met Gareth)
Gareth is really nice. Very funny and seems to have a good personality. We seem to have the same taste in music and values and I've given him my mobile number. He's going to ring me tomorrow night at 8.00pm. I'll check in then. Please Cupid, don't miss this time.

Tuesday
Cupid, you utter bastard. Why me? What have I ever done to you? I've just had a conversation with Captain Mainwaring from Dad's Army. The man in the photo surely can't be the same man who spoke 'at' me tonight. Please don't tell me it is. Someone needs to remind Gareth that he's not in the army anymore and that I'm not one of his platoon. 'So, what do you do in the MOD Gareth?' 'I can't tell you that, phones have ears and it's all very confidential'. 'Mine doesn't but that's fine if you can't tell me'. I did an awful thing then, pulled a face at my phone and cut him off. Even then he didn't take the hint and phoned me back. 'Sorry Gareth, the battery went in my phone'. 'That's okay, as long as you didn't cut me off on purpose'. 'No, not at all, it's nice to talk to you'. For fuck's sake Sarah, grow some balls and be honest, you don't owe this man anything. I've arranged to meet him on Saturday. I must be completely and utterly mad.

Saturday (making an effigy of Cupid.)
I'm embarrassed to even write in you this evening Di. It's 10.00pm, and I'm home already. I should be out laughing, flirting and revealing 'the girls' to my potential new love. Why am I not

I hear you ask? Because I've just met Giant Fucking Haystacks, that's why. Gareth, or 'lard arse' as he could also be known, was standing on the steps of the pub in a black Mac, black trousers and a white shirt, open at the neck (probably because it wouldn't do up). The Mac was undone, again, probably because it wouldn't do up. Hell Gareth, what's happened to you? Is what I wanted to say, but I just smiled and said it was nice to meet him.

He opened the door for me and we walked into the bar. It was a busy pub and I felt embarrassed to walk in with him. How awful, but I was so cross with him because I would have bet my last pound that I was meeting someone different. I have no problem with big men, but what I did have a problem with was the fact that he dropped into the conversation that his photo was seven years old. 'Yes, that photo was taken the day before I broke my back. I was in hospital for weeks and put on a lot of weight, but I've managed to do well and lose five stone'. I nearly spat my coke out because he had been even bigger! The lovely forearms I fell in love with in his photo now resembled thighs and I was so disappointed.

We sat down and Gareth looked uncomfortable. However, he made me feel thin. The buttons on his shirt were holding on for dear life and I was waiting for them to just give up and ping off into the open fire, which incidentally was making Gareth sweat profusely by now. Even though he couldn't talk about his job because it was just so top secret and he'd have to kill me, he still managed to dominate the evening with his ramblings. I managed a quick look at my watch and saw that I'd only been there for an hour. Oh God, surely my watch had stopped as it felt like I'd been here for a week. It was 8.00pm. I somehow managed another hour of boring conversation from Gareth talking about his job, accident, children, dog and some other crap I forget as I had now developed an unhealthy interest in the goings on of the four people on the table next to me.

I was brought back to 'Gareth's world' when I realised he was telling me something, which made him laugh out loud. It shocked me a bit but as I didn't have a bloody clue what he was talking about I just laughed too, thinking Oh God, I hope I'm okay to laugh! I eventually yawned and made my excuses to leave. Gareth walked me to my car and I leapt straight in wishing him a safe journey home and tearing off out of the car park.

Have texted friends and have agreed a strategy for next time. They are going to come with me and drive the 'lead car'. I will be waiting in a concealed location ready for the authority to proceed or not. They will observe the 'target' and perhaps even strike up a conversation with him if the need arises. They can either then radio in 'Strike, strike, strike!' or 'Abort mission. Repeat. Abort mission.' So, dwarf number five duly found, got rid of, and named 'Weeble' (because they wobble and don't fall down and I truly believe that would have happened to Gareth). Glass of wine Sarah? Yes please Di, I won't say no.

Thursday, November.

Have joined another website! Effigy of cupid is making me feel so much better though. I'm so bored and a friend recommended this site to me. The evenings are the worst and it's just nice to have some male company, if only of the virtual kind. There are the usual 'knob heads' on there, clearly out for sex. Anyway, a guy called Lee has caught my eye. I've given him 7/10 for looks. Luckily he has quite a few photos on his profile. Have learnt since Goofy to never fall for a man with only one photo, especially if it's a head shot and they're not smiling!

Saturday (I'm sure this time, honestly I am, Lee is the man of my dreams).

Lee and I are getting on so well. He was away for two nights this week and I was climbing the walls with boredom. I really did miss our chats and the way he makes me feel important and attractive. We 'meet' every night in a private chat room for , or as

Mum said, quite innocently the other day 'Get me a Celebrity I'm out of here'. It's like having him in the room with me. He's so funny and I love it. We 'talk' all the way through and take the Mickey out of the celebrities. It is just so refreshing to talk to a man and actually enjoy the conversation, knowing that it isn't all just a cunning plan to get in your pants.

Lee's wife had been having an affair and Lee had named him 'scrawny arse'. He was apparently very thin and smoked liked a chimney. He had the stained fingers and bad teeth to prove it, and drove a lorry. His daughter, Tamsin, who is ten, stays with him half the week. She's taken very well to the split and is desperate for her Dad to find a new woman. I've found out so much about him tonight and I'm going to bed with a smile on my face. Come on Cupid. If you make this 'the one' I promise I'll stop sticking pins in you.

Thursday
Lee sent me his mobile number. I just need to pluck up courage to actually text.

Sunday
Went out with the girls last night, got drunk and rang Lee. I have no idea what we said as I was tired and drunk. Not a good combination. He texted me though and said it was nice to talk to me at last and hoped that I wasn't feeling too hung-over today. Please God don't let me have said that I was feeling horny and hadn't had sex in a very long time.

Friday
We're going to meet up! Lee's coming to the house for a drink tonight when Jo-Jo's in bed. I'm very excited. Mum, however, is not happy that I'm doing this and would feel much better if I wore a panic button and had the police helicopter hovering ahead and the Royal Marines in the garden. 'I'll check in when

he's gone I promise, Mum'.

Lee is just lovely. Quite tall and stocky/solid but he has the loveliest kind face I've ever seen on a man. I joked with him and said that I had to keep sending 'I'm okay, he's not killed me' texts to my Mum. 'That's fine Sarah, I totally understand, and I do appreciate you letting me see you tonight. I love your company and would very much like to see you again'; 'I'd like that too Lee, you make me laugh and have my sense of humour'. We got on so well and there was definite sexual tension between us. He smelt nice too.

Tuesday (Post Christmas merriments and millions of texts from Lee)
It's a bit chilly up here on Cloud nine but who cares. I have a new man. Have put effigy of Cupid away, he deserves a break. I've decided not to rush things with Lee. Christmas came and we texted each other all the way through. It was his first Christmas on his own and so I texted him as soon as I woke up on Christmas morning. He's coming over on Sunday with Tamsin to go for a walk. Desperate to see each other. I hope Jo-Jo likes him.

Monday
Yesterday went really well. Tamsin is lovely and was so sweet to Jo-Jo. Jo-Jo really likes Lee too as he's a Star Wars fan and Jo-Jo pretends he's Luke Skywalker. Watching the two of them fighting with imaginary light sabres is hilarious.

Monday, February, 2010.
Evening Di. Can't believe I've not updated you for nearly six weeks! Things are going okay, ish.

Lee came up for the weekend but I'm finding faults now and realised I have rushed into things, and gone off him. He arrived on Saturday morning, armed with his own pillow. Not a great turn on. I'd bought us some cakes to eat to break the ice. Lee was very nervous. I'm the first woman he's been out with since he split from his wife. We had a lovely day, walking around town, like normal couples do. I felt in the majority for once instead of Billy no Boyfriend. Went clothes shopping for Lee and I had great fun picking out tops and chinos etc for him to wear. His wardrobe consisted of a vile Hawaiian shirt, a blue shirt from the eighties and one pair of jeans. Not good. He had a couple of t-shirts but they'd seen much better days. Looking at Lee in the changing room I was slightly concerned at his shape! Who am I to talk? I'm no supermodel, but I'm very quick to judge and all I could think of when I saw Lee was Oh my God he looks like a chicken. Nice enough legs, rock hard arse, but quite a big tummy and no hair on his chest apart from what I could only describe as a light dusting around the nipples. I think my arms were bigger than his. A slight panic set in, because I wasn't physically attracted to him. Oh bloody hell Sarah, you've done it again – judged someone before you've even got to know them. Practise what you preach woman, and look beyond the body.

Lee spent £80 on his new wardrobe and was very happy with his purchases. We ordered an Indian takeaway and I decided I needed to have some wine, as I was feeling a bit tense. Lee was such a laugh and we had a really good evening. What I really love about being with a man is just sitting, having a meal, drinking wine and being able to eat at my own pace, rather than the usual must eat dinner quickly, Jo-Jo has swimming in half an hour or I need to put the washing out before I go to bed and clean so need to wolf down dinner now.

We 'retired' to the lounge after dinner, feeling very full and more than slightly tipsy! Lee had bought some CDs with him. I'm not the best collector of music and what CDs I do have don't necessarily end up in the right cases; you could be very much in the mood for Keane and end up with Enya. Anyway, Lee put on Chicago and dimmed the lights a little bit. Lee leaned in and started kissing me. Delicious kisser I have to say. You could tell from the kiss that he really wanted me. I leaned back on the sofa and Lee moved in. I thought it was time to do my usual 'cop a feel'. Not bad. Not brilliant, but not bad. We were both feeling very horny. Let's be honest here, he hadn't had sex for months and months and neither had I, so combine alcohol and two sex starved people and what else does one expect?

But it all went horribly wrong. We could only do it successfully in one position i.e. on all fours as Lee kept popping out. Whilst he thought I was screaming with pleasure, it was more of a frustrated Why me again! He's not overly experienced, I appreciate that, but saying, 'Here we go!' when he came isn't a real turn on either. I couldn't help but notice his really hairy arse as well. Come Christmas he'll be able to hang baubles and fairly lights off it. Not great. I've reached a certain time in my life and really won't settle for second best. Why should I? I don't need a man, but would like one. There's a difference. I can't have a relationship with a man who doesn't do it for me. Will I ever get it right? I seem to keep making such stupid mistakes.

Thursday, April.

Lee stayed over with me again last night. He lives about an hour away so it's nice to see him once during the week. He turns up with his pillow and cooks me chicken korma and rice and we drink wine. The novelty is wearing off though, and the pinnacle of this was when he came up and changed into his tracksuit bottoms, tatty t-shirt and sat drinking whilst I cooked dinner last night. He and Jo-Jo sit on the sofa watching Star Wars. Jo-Jo adores him and it's so lovely seeing him enjoying Lee's company, but I'm having nagging feelings and I'm not happy.

Wednesday

Get this, I'm fuming. Lee's downstairs watching The Apprentice and I'm up in bed watching Will & Grace. We may as well be bloody married. I'm livid. I want romance. He never suggests anything! The weekends that I'm Jo-Jo free, all we do is stay at each other's houses. Feeling a bit claustrophobic. Life can be tedious when you're responsible for a child and having to think ahead all the time with them i.e. what am I doing for dinner? Is his school uniform clean for tomorrow? What after school club is it tonight? Lee isn't assertive enough for me. I have a small child to think off 24/7 so can't be arsed to think what Lee and I are going to do at the weekend. I need someone to say something like 'Right Sarah, you're child free this weekend, so we're going for lunch on the Moors and a night of sex at mine'.

Monday

It's been three days since I was sterilised and I really need to tell you all about it Di. I've been too knackered, and a bit sore, to muster up the strength to write, but oh my God I feel I've put to bed some post birth ghosts. Let me explain. I arrived at the hospital at 8.30am. Sue was having Jo-Jo for me so I had no childcare worries thankfully. It's not very comfortable though sitting in the waiting area, with no make up on, wearing nothing but a dressing gown! Anyway, I went in to the pre op room and put on the back to front gown and lay on the bed whilst they prepared everything. I kept comparing this to my labour. When I was taken for my c-section I was pretty much out of it with exhaustion and couldn't take in where I was. However, this time I was able to process who people were, what they were doing and think about what lay ahead of me. Exhaustion is a key factor to depression I believe but before I had my anaesthetic I was alert and fully in control. When I woke up, the first words I heard were 'Sarah, wake up, would you like some tea and toast?' 'Not yet thanks, I need more sleep'. Post birth I remember waking up to a midwife saying something like 'your baby's hungry and needs feeding'. In hindsight, how can you be expected to wake up from an anaesthetic and turn into Super Mum? Where does this expectation come from? Post sterilisation I was treated like royalty and allowed to sleep and come round in my own time.

The nurses were very attentive and brought me tea and toast, pure nectar. 'Just take your time Sarah and sit up when you're ready. Don't move too much and we'll get the doctor to come and give you the once over'. It's sad that no one said that to me when Jo-Jo was born. I had half of the midwifery team talking at me and pulling my boobs off trying to show me how to breastfeed. There was no consideration given to what I'd been through because, like I said before, billions of women have given birth, but that doesn't mean to say that these billions of women should adapt straightaway does it? Whilst I was waiting to be picked up by Mum, I cried a little, not because I can't have any more children, but because a ghost had reared it's ugly head today and I sent it packing. I feel very proud of the way I've recovered from Post Traumatic Stress and depression. If I'd had someone to talk to a couple of hours, or days even, after Jo-Jo was born, I think I'd have recovered a lot quicker. I wish the hospitals would let me visit women they think are suffering and just talk to them and, more importantly, listen to their stories. Feeling a bit tearful today, anaesthetic wearing off probably and body is getting back to normal, but at least I've got time to recover from this and process what I've been though. A new Mum has to get on with it and there just isn't time to think. Therefore, thoughts that aren't processed will 'splinter' and just get worse.

Sunday (Cottage Pie)

I was supposed to drive to Lee's for the evening for a change of scenery yesterday. I've been off all week recovering and because my stomach is still bloated, all I can get into is tracksuit bottoms. Even a week later, I'm not feeling up to driving to see Lee and feel frumpy in my tracksuit bottoms. He offered to come up and I was grateful for that and he said he'd sort dinner. I had my heart set on an Indian takeaway. I heard Lee's car arrive and saw him walk up to the house carrying a homemade sodding cottage pie. I know, I sound really ungrateful. I think what bugs me most is that, only after few months, we are like a married couple. Where was the romance? The alarm bells are ringing again and getting on my nerves. I have tried to make them stop but they just aren't having any of it. Lee is needy and I realise that he's one of those people who can't be without someone. Some people have to have someone in their life. I thought I was like that, but realise that I've been on my own for a while now and won't settle for someone I deem to be second best. Why have a mini volcano erupting in your ear whilst sleeping and two inches of the bed when you can have peace and quiet and lie like a star fish?

Monday

Lee came up again on Saturday and we just sat in front of the telly, eating chicken korma and drinking wine and cider and watching a DVD in our tracksuit bottoms – oh God its Wayne and Waynetta! We went to bed and I was thankful that my tummy was still sore so it prevented me from having sex with him. That's bad – we should still be at the ripping each other's clothes off stage and having sex all over the house.

Yesterday, I was bored beyond belief. Lee was watching yet another DVD and gobbling biscuits. I was like a coiled spring and didn't want to spend my Sunday afternoon doing nothing. I decided to go into the garden and Lee said he'd help. I wanted to scream at him, just do something, take me out, and decide what we should do for a change I have one child to look after I don't want another one. I know that sounds harsh, but why couldn't he have just whisked me off to the cinema or a walk along the beach? Anything, just suggest something, please!

The tension mounted between us that afternoon and he could tell I wasn't happy. Jo-Jo came home from Chris's and Lee was sitting in the garden with his head in his hands. Very melodramatic I thought, but he eventually came in. He sat with Jo-Jo watching some more crap on the TV whilst I did some work on the computer. We hardly spoke to each other. When Jo-Jo went to bed, Lee and I settled down to watch yet more bloody TV, some murder mystery thing that neither of us were paying attention to. 'What's wrong Sarah? You've not been right for a while now'. 'I'm so sorry Lee, but this just isn't working for me. You're a lovely guy but I don't think we're suited. I think we've settled down too quickly and we're after different things. I think we should stop seeing each other'. Oh god, that didn't go down well, but I really couldn't lie to Lee. He packed his bags and left, saying that he'd ring me tomorrow. I feel awful now but I told him I didn't want to hear from him tomorrow because I won't change my mind and think it's for the best. Oh Di, he burst into tears and, okay, so I'm a bitch because instead of feeling sorry for him I just kept thinking *oh for fuck's sake be a man Lee and just leave me alone*. I turned off the TV went to bed, quite relieved that it was over. When I woke up this morning I'd had a missed call from Lee, but luckily my phone was on silent. Listening to the message it was clear he was in tears again, practically begging me to take him back. I phoned him and said that it was my fault, not his. I'm further down the line than him, in as much as I've been single longer than him and his divorce is still so raw for him. He's struggling to be on his own and I think he's panicking about it a bit. We had a good chat and I thanked him for all his support over the last couple of weeks (I'm not completely without heart) and that he was a great guy, but I just wanted to be on my own.

Jo-Jo was gutted when I told him that Lee had gone to work in Scotland and we wouldn't be seeing him again for a long time. What a liar, but how could I explain to my child that I've finished with Lee because he had a hairy arse, walked like a pregnant chicken and had about as much get up and go as a popped balloon. Jo-Jo then suggested we fly up to Scotland to see Lee. Bloody hell! I'm hoping he'll forget about it, but if not I may have to say he's been promoted and is now working in Alaska! Am going to block myself from all Internet dating sites and donate £100 to charity each time I fall off the Internet dating wagon. I don't want to give Lee a 'dwarf' name, but I'm getting into the swing of naming them all now and feel he'd like one! He's going to be called 'Hairy'.

Wednesday, May.
Before you start laughing and preaching at me, I am fully aware of what I said about the Internet. I don't have £100 at the moment and, quite frankly, it's my life and I think everything should be done in threes, it's supposed to be lucky, so this is my lucky third go, okay?

Have been communicating with Stewart, or 'Stew' as he likes to call himself. He actually seems a really nice guy. Yes, I know they all do to begin with, but his photo looked very natural. He is also very funny and it's important that we can have a laugh. He has a slight tummy on him, shaven head, and looks quite huggable. He's in the navy and has a son the same age as Jo-Jo. We're going out for a drink on Sunday when Jo-Jo is with Dad of the year.

Submarine Sunday
How can I ever show my face in public again? Stewart texted me, not phoned, texted, to say that the submarine's broken down in port and he has to stay on and try and fix it. I didn't believe him to be honest and so spent the day clothes shopping to cheer myself up because despite all my early optimism, I've obviously met another twat.

Friday
Stewart eventually phoned and we've made arrangements to go out for a drink in Torquay. 'I'm really sorry about the weekend Sarah, but honestly the sub broke down and she's my baby so I just had to stay and look after her'. I acted very nonchalantly about the whole thing, never give too much away I've come to realise. Anyhow, went out for a drink with Stewart on

Wednesday. Wasn't nervous and decided to really make an effort. No one stands me up for a submarine without regretting it. I strolled into the pub and he was stood at the bar. Inside, and to coin one of my Mum's phrases I was 'shitting bricks' but the exterior oozed confidence. He wasn't bad looking and even looked like his photo! The evening went on and we seemed to be sat in the hub of the weekly pub quiz. We joined in and had a laugh about how obviously unintelligent we were. Stewart was nice, quite shy, but I could work on that. The evening ended and we said our goodbyes, the bit I hate, as you know. 'Would you like to do this again?' he asked and I obviously said yes.

Saturday (one week on)
No matter how much I checked my phone for hidden/lost texts by banging it, taking out the battery and sim card and getting friends to text me to ensure the phone was working, there was nothing from Stewart. I'm thoroughly pissed off to be honest. I know I could have text him, but he's asked me out again in a roundabout way so I don't like to. How dare he.

Friday
Texted Stewart last night in drunken haze. No reply. Really hacked off as I thought we'd got on well.

Thursday
I've had random texts from Stewart saying 'Hi, how are you?' I've not replied to any of them and have removed his number from my phone to save me from drunken texting in the future.

Sunday
I logged onto the website and saw Stewart was online so decided to email him. I need to write down what was said word for word because I may need it in the future but mainly because I know I will want to keep reading it. I started…

'Hi Stranger, how are you?'

'Hi Sarah, I'm good thanks, how's life treating you?'

'Great thanks. Just answer me one question, why did you go quiet on me and not contact me again?'

'You don't want to know.'

'Yes I do, so please tell me.'

'Okay, well you did ask. Your photo was completely different to how you looked in reality. Your hair was slightly different and on our date you were wearing glasses'. I read this at least three times as I couldn't believe what he'd said. After a big gulp of wine and a five-minute rant, I sent him a reply.

'Oh Stewart, you are funny; but now it's my turn to tell you what I actually felt, but chose to overlook. You were obviously wearing trousers three sizes too big, which in turn made me concerned that you'd forgotten to bring your arse with you as there was just no sign of one (but you obviously do have one as your head is apparently stuck up there). There was an obvious hint of a man boob through your cheap, unflattering super-market jumper, and if I heard one more story about your fucking submarine and how precious she was to you, I was going to scream. However, I chose to give you a second chance. Finally, as regards the fact that I'd styled my hair ever so slightly differently to my profile picture, which was only six months old, all I can reply to that is at least I have some. There is no way a shallow arsehole like you will/could ever squash my confidence. Your comments actually made me laugh. You should have considered yourself lucky to be seen with me. Talk about beauty and the beast.'

With that I blocked Stewart from ever contacting me again, logged off and shut down my computer feeling satisfied that I'd prevented him from trying to have the last word. No man will ever squash my confidence and try and put their insecurities and lack of confidence on to me. Girl Power! He will now be known as 'Moobe' (as in 'man boob' – I love it!).

So, Snow White has met her seven dwarfs! Goofy, Twitcher, Tosspot, Dickless, Weeble, Hairy and Moobe. I now just need my Prince, please! Could I ever live with another man? As I lie here in my double bed, I realise just how set in my ways I've become. I lie diagonally, legs and arms sprawled out not wanting to miss any opportunity to use up the bed space. I've got into the habit of listening to Classic FM too to send me off to sleep. I'm not finding it easy to get to sleep tonight though, despite being so extremely cosy and I've started to think, could I ever live with another man? Have I become too independent, self-reliant or set in my ways?

Chapter 10

Me, Myself and Jo-Jo

The reason women don't play football is because eleven of them would never wear the same outfit in public.
Phyllis Diller

Wednesday, June (School Olympics)
Jo-Jo's in bed and told me tonight that he's looking forward to sports day tomorrow as it means time out of the classroom. I smiled and said that it didn't matter what happens during his races, it's the taking part that counts. And I told him to have some fun and cheer on his classmates. His sports day has brought back so many memories for me. I hated it when I was his age. In fact I hated anything that involved physically exerting myself. I wasn't fat as a child, I prefer to think of myself as 'big-boned', but I was always bigger than my friends, in width and height. Think of Big Foot and The Henderson's, with me obviously playing the lovable, but slightly awkward 'Big Foot', and you get the general idea.

I remember nearly getting stuck in a hoop during one race. It was a combination of trying to master the art of stepping in to the hoop and getting it over my head and also my body size not giving the hoop much room for manoeuvre. I'm sure I heard one wince when I approached it mid race, sweat pouring from having run five metres. Anyway, I digress, but because of my lack of enthusiasm for anything sporty, I'm not in the least bit competitive or excited about the impending reception sports day. It's just a nice morning out of work to watch a bunch of four and five year olds enjoying themselves for an hour or two and a chance for a gossip with the Mums, right?

Wrong. My attitude isn't shared by all. I overheard two Mums in the playground on Monday and tried so hard not to laugh.

'I don't know what's wrong with George, he's normally really good at running. He came second in the practise race on Friday. I think he's tired'.

'I know, Jack's the same, I just hope he's okay on the day, otherwise he'll be gutted'.

In other words, they'll be gutted. I wonder what their reaction would have been if I had nonchalantly said that Jo-Jo had been having training from a personal coach and had been on a strict protein diet for a month! Stupid women. It's a sports day for five year olds. This isn't the Olympics with live coverage from the BBC and commentary from Linford Christie. Really, these women need to stop taking it so seriously and get a life!

Thursday

I think I need to find a new school for Jo-Jo; In Canada. Sue and I were so bloody early on Sports Day, we felt we ought to help the staff put out the chairs. I've reached the conclusion that if I were ever reincarnated, it would be best if it weren't as a rooster. My dawn chorus would get earlier and earlier, for fear of being late and I'd probably end up being shot for *cockadoodle-doodling* at 3.00am. Sue and I pitched up in the front ready for the races to start. All the children trotted out and my Jo-Jo was in the first running race. There were eight of them all ready to run. Suddenly, I could feel myself morphing into 'Psycho Mum'. My pulse started racing and I was trying to catch Jo-Jo's eyes to give him some words of encouragement but he was too busy laughing with his friends. I was getting cross because he should have been concentrating. This was no time for a laugh. He could win this. He was good at running and won the nursery running race last year.

I suddenly developed ants in my pants and couldn't decide if I should stand up, sit down or crouch on the side of the track. I was sussing out the competition and realised that the tall boy next to him would be his closest rival. I hoped the grass was uneven in his lane and that he would stumble. How sad is that? The whistle blew and Jo-Jo started a split second behind the others, as he didn't quite hear the whistle. My new found competitiveness was in full flow. I was shouting so fiercely that I could feel the veins standing out in my neck. 'Come on Jo-Jo you can win this, run sweetheart, run'. He came a very close second and I know that, until the end of time, I will always be peeved because they didn't restart the race for him; he would have come first you know.

I sat down and heard a woman behind me say to her friend, 'She was a bit over the top'. But that was just the start. Then came the egg and spoon race. I actually half stood and half sat and waved frantically at Jo-Jo. He looked at me in a confused way because I was trying to demonstrate to him how to hold the spoon! I'm ashamed to admit to this, but after the egg fell off for the third time and Jo-Jo was trailing in fourth place, my psycho emotions got the better of me and I actually shouted, 'Hold the egg on the spoon Jo-Jo'. It was at this point I felt I ought to calm down a bit, otherwise I had visions of being man handled off the school grounds for encouraging my child to cheat!

It was time for the parents' races and this is when I should have left. This is why I need to emigrate. Sue told me to enter as she knew I had this urge to rid myself of bad childhood memories of sports days gone by. Well, all of them actually. Jo-Jo shouted at me to join in and all his friends cheered me on too. I was pumped up with adrenalin by this stage, jumping up and down to warm up, and still in 'Psycho Mum' mode. Gone was the attitude that it was a nice morning off work, a chance to catch up with friends and spend a relaxing time in the sun watching Jo-Jo have fun. This was war on a grand scale. I was the first one up on the touch line and eyed up the competition. I was confident I could have them. One Mum was considerably shorter than me, as were her legs and the other looked as if she'd rather die than take part.

Then suddenly hundreds seemed to appear and my confidence deserted me. Why didn't I listen to my head and just walk off? No one would have noticed. I had to run in bare feet, without the aid of my ultra support sports bra, and a t-shirt, which kept falling off my shoulder at the best of times. 'On your marks ladies, get set, GO'. I started running but didn't seem to be going anywhere. I had heard Jo-Jo and his friends cheering me on but all I could see were the backs of other Mums overtaking me at lightning speed. I'd kept my sunglasses on too and seemed to lose all sense of direction. I just about managed to keep myself up right and not fall over with the shock of such exertion. By the time I finished, my boobs had escaped from my bra and were jumping around all over the place enjoying their new found freedom and I needed oxygen, fast. I tried so hard to laugh it all off, but deep down it was like being at primary school all over again. I came ninth. There were only ten of us in the race and the woman I beat had her right arm in a sling. Oh the shame of it. So, not only did I manage to resurrect painful memories of sports days gone by, I've now created all new, even more humiliating ones. Well done Sarah!

Tuesday (Twenty Questions)
I nearly blew a gasket today. Jo-Jo thinks I know everyone, everywhere in the whole world. Not only that, but he seems to think I know what they're doing, when, where and why. On the way to school this morning, a man was walking, minding his own business. I didn't notice him, I'm a parent with endless tasks swirling around in my head and it was only 8.15am. We drove past him and Jo-Jo pipes up 'Why is that man walking down the road?' In my 'pause the world' moment where no one can hear me, I shout How the fuck would I know? so loudly that my voice box bruises. I then reverse the car back at 80mph and actually ask the man why indeed he is walking down the road at 8.15am

minding his own business.

However, in the real world, I just miss out the word 'fuck'. The scream is still fever pitch because I really don't know how many times I can cope with him asking me things like 'Is everyone at school going to the party on Saturday?' 'Why is that lady riding her bike?' 'Why is the sky blue?' 'Is Jack at school today?' My life is devoid of much adult conversation as it is, so having questions like that thrust at me before 8.30am is just murderable. Not sure if 'murderable' is a word, but today it is.

So Di, I have devised my own little let off steam sheet. I am so surprised I have any knuckles left quite frankly due to the fact that I am constantly putting them in my mouth to stop something rude, sarcastic and inappropriate for the ears of a child, sprouting from my mouth. I think this expresses my new found sense of maturity and control and I have listed them as follows, firstly the 'question or statement' followed by response (A) What you actually say to your little darling then response (B) what you never say out loud, but your head is begging you to. Anyway, enjoy!

Q .Why are those children playing outside Mummy?

(A) Oh sweetheart, they're probably enjoying the lovely weather. It's nice to see them enjoying themselves.

B) *What? Why are you asking me? Am I their Mum?*

Q. Are there such things as ghosts Mummy?

(A) No, of course not darling. Now don't be afraid to go to sleep. I'll put teddy in the doorway so that he can protect you and blow all the nasty things away. Here's a big kiss from me too for extra protection. Goodnight sweetheart.

(B) Yes there are and if you call me again and interrupt me the naughty boy ghost will come and haunt you for making Mummy tired and irritable. Now bugger off and get to sleep.

Q. I'm not going to bed.

(A) But Jo-Jo you must my little munchkin as it's school tomorrow and you can't be tired for that now can you?

(B) Oh really? Get up those stairs now and get your backside in bed before I drag you up there at 80mph.

Q. The word 'why' in general, at the start of every sentence.

(A) Oh Jo-Jo I do love your inquisitive mind. Well done darling.

(B) For the love of God child stop asking 'Why?' at the start of every sodding sentence. You're driving me up the bloody wall. It's past 7.00pm and the shutters on Mummy's 'Why shop' are closed now. Please leave a message after the expletive.

Q. Where do babies come from?

(A) From a woman's tummy. Daddies kiss the Mummies' tummy and give it a big cuddle and wish a baby to grow inside.

(B) Asda

Q. When will we die?

(A) Oh Jo-Jo, when it's our time to. God will take us when he needs us. We must put our trust in him.

(B) Am I still alive?

Thursday, July.

House is too small. When Jo-Jo has the TV on all you can hear are the same programmes over and over again. Now that Jo-Jo is older, the programmes are slightly more bearable. He's into Ben 10 Alien Force, Sponge Bob Square Pants and Star Wars Clone Wars. I realised just how sad and bored I am when I had to look up the words to Ben 10 today whilst cooking in the kitchen, as there was one part where I couldn't quite understand what they were saying and it was annoying me because I couldn't sing along to the whole song! Yes, Di, I know, I have no life, at least none I can call my own. I have no idea what's happening in the outside world. All I know is that Ben 10 has had a fight with Vilgax, Anakin Skywalker has turned into Darth Vader and I've had to pretend to be Obi Wan. Please make the noises stop and tell me that there is a life outside of children's TV.

Mmmmm Monday.

Please ignore my selfish and intolerant rant about Jo-Jo's TV programmes. I need to learn to share and take an interest in what he enjoys. Which is what I did today. Bloody hell why has no one told me about Deadly Sixty before now? Can I buy the series on DVD? Jo-Jo called me into the lounge for the twelfth time during my attempt at cooking a Lasagne without letting the white sauce go lumpy. 'Mum look at this snake'. For fuck's sake, I'm cooking. 'Hang on Jo-Jo, I'm trying to cook…' and then I saw him. Sod the white sauce this is a sight to behold. The programme, Deadly Sixty, hosted by a drop dead gorgeous and rugged man who fights snakes and lives rough in the undergrowth looking for deadly animals. I really must watch Deadly Sexy again.

Tuesday, August.

Another thing you have to learn as a single Mum, with a son, is not only how to tolerate football, but to actually learn to play it. It's compulsory. I was always more of a rugby fan, far better thighs and it has a better status to it somehow. From an early age, Jo-Jo has always enjoyed kicking a ball around and I've had to learn how to enjoy it as much as he does. Jo-Jo's love of football is becoming more and more apparent, so I've decided to enrol him in the local football club. He was so excited about going but felt a little frustrated that he didn't have any kit to wear like all the other boys. I just sent him in a t-shirt, shorts and trainers. I'm not forking out for the kit for him to announce, two weeks later, 'I don't want to go again, it's not my thing'. Oh yes, this has happened before with Karate so forgive my scepticism. We arrived at the playing field and there was no time for me to assess the situation. I spotted the men in charge though, who were all wearing the local club strip. Two were young enough to be my sons and the other old enough to be my father. It was like I was running the gauntlet walking up to them 'Hello, I'm Sarah, Jo-Jo's Mum, I phoned about bringing Jo-Jo up for a trial'.

'Oh yes, I remember' said the older man. 'Hello Jo-Jo, nice to see you. Dave here will take you over for a warm up with the other newer players. Mum you can either stay and watch or go and do your shopping and come back later if you like'. Go and do your shopping? Blasted cheek. If that had been a man he'd have probably said go to the gym or have a pint. I know it was my paranoia, but I felt so conspicuous. Everyone there was male. I was the only female amongst, say, thirty Dads and nearly forty children.

This club is called 'Footie Tots', emphasis being on the word 'Tots'. The boys are very young; however, if you could have just seen the Dads' reactions to how their sons were playing. I stupidly looked around to make sure there weren't any cameras and that I wasn't standing on the sidelines of Wembley stadium. One Dad was 6ft tall, rather skinny, wearing an Everton top over ill-fitting jeans and new white trainers. Although it was late summer, I thought it was rather chilly, but men being men can't feel the cold and they stand on the side lines in just a 'footie' shirt pretending they're not cold. He was watching his son so intently 'Lewis, attack the ball'. 'Where's the support Lewis?' 'Tackle him Lewis' were just a few things his very supportive and encouraging Dad called to the poor boy. Lewis was obviously spending too much time listening to his Dad's 'instructions' and couldn't concentrate on what the paid coach was telling him, because he was tackled and missed a goal. Dad was not happy.

Then there was Owen's Dad. 'Keep your eye on the ball Owen and concentrate lad'. Further along was Michael's Dad', short, fat bloke who looked like he could have been a football let alone play it. According to his 'loving' contributions, poor old Michael wasn't paying attention, or defending enough, generally being of no use at all. I was amazed by their reactions. These boys are between four and seven years old. At one point I was concerned one of them would hyper ventilate with sheer frustration at the way their potential little football star in the kit of his Dad's choosing, was playing. Dads, please remember this is a hobby, emphasis on 'hobby' – H.O.B.B.Y. We are at a local school playing field on a Thursday evening. What part of this environment makes you think we're at Wembley? And there is no prize money at stake here, no transfer fees, you do realise that, don't you?

Jo-Jo thoroughly enjoyed his evening and couldn't wait to go again. This meant walking into a sports shop to buy 'the kit'. I hate sports shops. Full of young boys with spiked up, gelled hair, wearing Fred Perry shirts with the collar up and the latest trend in jogging bottoms. When I asked about buying an England strip I nearly passed out. A pair of shorts, top and socks was going to set me back over £50. The look of 'you're having a laugh' was written on my face and the boy in the shop showed me a better deal, which was still very expensive.

Then came the trainers. The 'boy' assistant took me over to the trainers. 'What are you looking for?' No offence, but do I look like I know? 'I need football boots that combine playing outside and inside'. Crap description but what else could I say? Having just spent my food money on the kit, the cheaper the better We settled for a pair of run of the mill trainers, which were thankfully in the sale. I left there two weeks' food money lighter, working out how I was going to cope now, but with a little boy who was skipping with happiness back to the car carrying the bag with his new football kit in it. He spent the rest of the day in it and I let him go to bed wearing it too. It was worth being short of money for.

I'm a single Mum, supporting her son and proud of it. I may not know the offside rule, nor do I really care. I looked it up on the Internet once. There was even a girlie explanation of it about being in a shoe shop and two women spotting the same pair of shoes. That would never happen in my world, I Internet shop mostly and I still couldn't grasp it. So, I have made up my own version of it, which is far easier to understand. Think of how competitive we all get when it's school play time. We want to be first in the queue to get in. My attitude is it's taken me blood sweat and tears to ensure Jo-Jo looks good as a donkey in his nativity play and by God I'm going to ensure that I have a darned good view of his performance.

So, Di, here is Sarah Chilton's explanation of the offside rule, so pay attention please! The nativity starts promptly at 10.00am. You arrive at 9.33am precisely. You walk to the office with a slight smug smile on your face assuming you'll be the first. Shock horror, there's another Mum in front of you. Damn it. The school reception waiting area is slowly starting to fill. The head teacher is standing behind the doors ready to open them at 9.55am. He stands there for a while. You suddenly realise you've left your ticket for the nativity play of the century in the car. The Mum in front of you sees the look of horror on your face and she then frantically searches for her ticket. She's forgotten hers too. You both look at each other with the head teacher still poised behind the door.

Your traditionally late friend arrives. She's half way down the queue. You mouth to her I've forgotten my bloody ticket. She mouths back I've got a spare one, Mum can't come. Get ready to catch my bag (which would be the ball!). She throws it, and as you catch it the head teacher is just opening the door, which then means you can walk past the first lady and be first through the door. However, if your friend lobbed the bag in front of Mum number one you could nip in front of her and get through the door. But, until the bag has actually left your friend's hands, it would be rude for you to be in front of Mum number one, hence being offside. There, easy!

In order for Jo-Jo to improve his football skills, he needs to practise, which is where I come in, unfortunately. Tips:

1. When going to a public place to practise with your son, always wear a supportive bra. There is nothing worse than running to get the ball with your boobs wobbling around

like two puppies in a sack.

2. Never wear open toe shoes. I am still paying the price; the nail on my big toe is growing back slowly.

3. Kick with the side of the foot, otherwise, number 2 will happen if you're not wearing trainers.

4. Don't ever attempt 'keepy uppies' in a public place. Your child will die ashamed.

5. If you ever score a goal, don't do what Jayne did once and pull your top over your head, like footballers do, unless you've adhered to point 1.

Sunday

Fan-bloody-tastic, I'm going to be in the Centre Parcs club! So many of my friends talk about this wonderful place of tranquillity, serenity and relaxation, I can't wait. Mum and I are taking Jo-Jo and his friend Will. I've booked archery and fencing for the boys and lots of relaxing and drinking wine for me and Mum. I hope the weather's nice. The adverts make the place look so happy and carefree. I'm so excited! I've got two weeks to prepare and I'm so looking forward to the break and relaxation for three nights whilst the boys place in the woods and entertain themselves.

Tuesday, October

Relaxing? Tranquil? Serene? You're having a laugh. I've never been so sodding exhausted in my life. Arrived, all excited, Jo-Jo and Will were hyper. We unloaded the luggage and I then drove car to the parking area and walked back. Bearing in mind we'd had a two-hour drive, I was pretty exhausted. We had a lovely meal out, Mum and I got a bit tipsy and she had to get on her knees and crawl on to the land train back to the cabin. I nearly wet myself! Then Saturday morning came and the words 'can we go swimming Mum?' were spoken. We got there as the pool opened. I say pool; it's like a mini village of pools and slides.

Quite frankly my idea of hell but you can't expect two children to tolerate a trip to the spa with Mummy and not go swimming can you? So, off we trot to the outside pool where the water slide from hell is situated. It saw me coming and thought we'll have her. We'd already watched people having a laugh on it the day before, which is why I got tipsy because I knew what was waiting for me the next morning. I'm not the world's most athletic person and I had to jump and hoist myself up on to the start of the rapids. This meant that the person behind me got an eyeful of my backside. Not a good start. I'm sure the bastards grease the slides. I hate water and at one point I managed to turn and end up going down headfirst, hit the water, and flapped around like a drowning beetle, trying to surface. Okay so it's only two foot deep but it was frightening. After the fourth time I thought the boys would have had enough and want to move onto something else. Oh no, add a zero onto that four and even then they still wanted more. If one more child pushed me, bumped into me or screamed in my face, I would have been arrested for murder by drowning. By the end of the day I had a bruised pelvis and burnt nose from the water shooting up it at 80mph. After four hours, I had actually lost the will to live. I'd been on the rapids forty five times as Jo-Jo wanted one last go. Stop laughing Di, it's really not funny. Then came the death slide and a green water shoot that was just horrible and very quick. Good for the tummy muscles though as I had to hold myself upright whilst travelling quicker than the speed of sound. I did that three times and couldn't fake smiling and enjoyment any longer. That wasn't the end of my 'relaxing' activities. Then came their fencing lesson. This was my time to collapse and recharge the batteries and watch them. But oh no, the cocky little shit taking the lesson saw that there were uneven numbers so he said, 'Would your Mum like to join in?' Bastard. Half an hour I had to endure of fencing with some feeble sponge like excuse for a sword. Mum and I cooked dinner for the boys when we got home and relaxed with two bottles of wine. It was beautiful weather and I couldn't move. Every bone, muscle, joint and ligament in my body was aching. Just get me my quilt and I'll sleep outside.

The boys didn't get to sleep until after 11pm and I thought they'd wake up later on the Sunday as they'd worn themselves out the day before. How stupid am I? 6.30am they woke up and decided to dance around, scream, laugh and pretend to be Ben bloody 10. I managed to have a shower and breakfast before being pleaded with to go swimming again. I needed a new pelvis and could hardly walk from mounting the bloody rapids, so how on earth I was going to endure another day of hell made me feel physically sick. I counted thirty five times of descending 'The Slide of Satan' and was shaking by the end of it. Di, stop laughing, it's not funny! We then got the land train home, with me not knowing what day of the week it was. I had my mouth open and eyes half shut and nearly fell off at one point. Don't let's even mention the archery. We walked there for Jo-Jo's tiredness to really kick in. Tears flowed when the arrow didn't hit the target or he kept dropping it. We walked home with him in tears, whilst I resembled a raging bull aiming for its target. I was supposed to be relaxing. I saw a sign for the Spa and could have cried. Jo-Jo had reached the peak of tired mountain and was coming back down the other side at a great speed of knots, taking everyone with him on the way. It wasn't pleasant. Then came the gift shop. How can one child spend so long in a shop the size of a small lounge? I should have taken a chair, book and glass of wine and let him get on with it. He had ten pounds to spend and it took an hour for him to decide. When I looked around, everyone else had families, Mums, Dads etc who looked happy. Why was I the only one who looked like I'd just completed the London Marathon? Monday was exhausting. Muscles still pissed off with me for putting them through such hell and so I was walking like I'd pooped my pants. I had to walk and get the car, load it up and drive home. I would rather have extracted my wisdom teeth with a blunt knife than do that. So Di, I'd rate my time at Centre Parcs, on a scale of 1-10 as being 6. I did manage to sit down at some point, even if it was to wipe my backside, but I now need a holiday. *Mental note Sarah, don't go again unless you have someone else who can swim.* Mind you, I lost 4lbs!

Thursday

I have yet another 'clear the air' chat with Chris to look forward to. Oh joy. It was Jo-Jo's assembly today. He was an Octopus. It's all come about since Jo-Jo came back and said he's bored when he goes to see Chris. My solicitor recommended I put all this in writing with suggestions of what Chris could do with Jo-Jo on his weekends with him. Chris phoned me and wants to meet with me after Jo-Jo's assembly. The assembly was brilliant and I'm so proud of Jo-Jo as he had to stand up and say 'Thank you all for coming and enjoy your day'. So sweet.

At the end we all go up and congratulate our children and Jo-Jo goes immediately to Chris, who picks him up in one hand and parades him around the hall. Jo-Jo loves it and makes Chris go up to his friends so that they can see his Dad and how strong he is. I'm outwardly smiling and pretending to be relaxed but deep down I just want to go home and get this over with. Jo-Jo gives Chris a hug and waves goodbye to me. Chris and I agree to meet at a coffee shop. 'You could come back to mine if you like for coffee, it's not so public'. 'No, I don't want to go to yours, I'll meet you at Sainsbury's coffee shop'. Great, this isn't going to go well judging by his attitude towards me.

We sit down at a table for two. 'Well Chris, this is a first for us since we split up, having a civilised coffee together.'

He just laughs and sits down. 'Right, I want to clear the air' and with that he pulls out what appeared to be his script, written by Hagrid (not in poisoned ink or on parchment paper though). Why did she have to write it? Has he lost the ability to use a pen or his brain? 'I think it's time to air my views and I want you to listen to me without interrupting'. At this point, I've already mentally poured my coffee all over him and rugby tackled him to the ground, but I sit and smile and let him get on with it. 'Mary and I were really annoyed at receiving your letter stating how our weekends with Jo-Jo should be spent. I'm almost wondering whether it's worth me bothering to see him. If he's not happy then why should I bother? I will not be dictated to by you on what I do and when I do it. My time with him is precious. I was pissed off quite frankly when you told me you'd changed his swimming to a Saturday morning. I do not want to come and see him swim; I think it's a waste of my time. Also, we don't see why you can't bring him up to us sometimes. Why should I do all the driving?'

By this time, I was more interested in watching the home shopping van being loaded, wondering what people had ordered, which then lead me on to what I was going to cook for dinner. I mentally entered Chris's space again and saw that he'd gone a blotchy red all over his face and neck, which means he was obviously nervous and angry at the same time! However, it wasn't his anger and this wasn't him speaking. This was Mary. Chris hasn't got the balls to do this. 'Also, when Joshua was born, I could have reduced my maintenance to you, but Mary and I had a chat about it and decided it wouldn't be fair on Jo-Jo, so we decided to keep it as it is. You mentioned in your letter that he gets upset because he can't bring his toys home that Mary, myself and our family have bought. We've spent our hard earned cash on those toys and don't see why you should get the benefit of them'.

'Okay Chris I've heard enough now. Firstly, you chose to have an affair. I don't want to know why, nor, after all this time, do I deserve to. Secondly, you also chose to live in a different county so why, on my weekend off, should I drive Jo-Jo up to see you when I've done nothing but put him first and ferry him around all over the place to school and his various hobbies all week. When you were having your cosy little affair you should have thought about the consequences of shagging another woman whilst your wife was pregnant. A pregnancy that had been planned by both of us despite what you told people. My life is devoted to Jo-Jo and his needs. Do you think I wanted to arrange swimming on a Saturday morning and get up at 'stupid o'clock' on a weekend? As for the maintenance Chris, if it means that much to you then reduce it. I've managed all this time without you, another few quid a month won't have an effect on me.'

'We may just do that.'

'God Chris, you're such an arse and really quite thick'. With that I storm out of the coffee shop, much to the annoyance of the people next to us who were having the time of their lives listening to what was being said. I, on the other hand, was seething at the arrogance of the man. Just carry on what you're doing Sarah, let the bastard have his rant. He's obviously under her thumb. What a twat. I don't think he expected that reaction from me. I was always doing things to please him and make sure he was happy. Bollocks to that now, he'll never try and bully me again. I've come a long way since he walked out.

Saturday, January, 2011.

Jo-Jo's off with Voldermort this weekend so I have some 'me' time without him saying 'Can I help Mummy?' It's great that he wants to do something for me, but flicking soil over the lawn and digging up flowers and leaving the weeds, isn't my idea of help. Anyway, Chris's attitude has annoyed me again just lately and we had a row about parents' evening. 'Why didn't you tell me it was Johnathan's parent's evening last week. I'm his Dad and entitled to go'. 'After your embarrassing outburst last time Chris and lack of interest in Jo-Jo's schooling, I didn't see the point in asking you'. Have I not told you about his embarrassing outburst? I must have told you about the bean incident, surely? Well, quickly then, cos it's relevant to what I did next!

I had a call from the school to say that Jo-Jo wasn't very well, seems to have started a cold and wants his Mum. Great, I thought, I was out shopping with Mum. It was a Friday and the day after her birthday. I picked him up at about 11.00am. 'He says his nose is sore and seems to be getting a cold but is very upset for some reason'.

'What's the matter Jo-Jo?' He was very sheepish.

'Nothing, I just don't feel well and my nose is sore'. It looked a bit puffy and mother's instinct told me he'd put something up it. 'I've not put anything up it' he said defiantly.

'Okay sweetie, but if you have, I won't be cross. I need to find out because whatever's up there needs to come out before it goes septic'. At this point, Jo-Jo started crying and told me that a bean from a bean bag fell up it. I refrained from laughing and took him, and Mum, to the hospital. Nine bloody hours and a general anaesthetic later, we came home, together with bean. I still have it as a memento!

Anyway, Chris came to parents' evening, having adopted his usual *I'm here everyone, look at me* attitude. We sat down to talk to Miss West, Johnathan's teacher. 'Nice to meet you Mr Chilton' she said.

'Thanks. Before we start, I'd like to find out more about this bean incident. I just wondered how this could have happened'. He was very forthright in his approach and quite brusque.

Has anyone got a sledge hammer and pneumatic drill please as I need to dig a very large hole. 'It's all been sorted Chris, we're here to talk about Jo-Jo's education'. I reminded him.

'Don't interrupt me, I have a right to know'. Sod the pneumatic drill, give me a gun. 'That's okay,' said Miss West looking really embarrassed by this point, 'unfortunately, one of the bean bags must have had a slight hole in it and children being children, decided to experiment shall we say'.

'I'm concerned how he was in possession of a bean bag with a hole.'

'Chris, this isn't nursery, the teachers can't be expected to 'mother' them all day'. I was so embarrassed for Miss West. The parents' evening continued and it was the longest ten minutes of my life. 'Thanks Miss West, I'll catch up with you tomorrow' and tried to discreetly give her an apologetic look. 'Don't ever behave like that again Chris. That behaviour was appalling. You made yourself look a right tit'. 'I had a right to know what happened to my son'. 'Of course you did Chris, but that wasn't the time or the place to do it. You can't pick and choose what you take an interest in. Don't treat Jo-Jo like he's one of your hobbies.' Unfortunately, the school hall is a long way to the exit and I was walking at least twenty feet in front of Chris and it felt like I was walking the green mile! So, the weekend after this disastrous parents' evening, I was still seething with Chris. Mum had bought Jo-Jo some wriggly worm sweets for his Friday evening treat. He loved them and are his favourite. 'I want to save one for Daddy tomorrow'.

'Okay darling, no problem. Leave them by the door and you won't forget to take them then'. That evening, and a few glasses of wine later, Mum and I were talking about Chris and the appalling way he'd behaved at parents' evening. 'What a prat' Mum said, 'he always has to think he's on top'.

'Oh Mum no reminders of sex with him please!'

'Oh Sarah, you know what I mean. He's always got to think he's got the upper hand'.

An hour later, after a full bottle of Chardonnay, I spotted the sweetie bag by the front door. 'I've had a wicked idea' I said to Mum and picked up the sweetie bag. I got out the two wriggly worms Jo-Jo had saved for Chris and wiped them in my armpit. I'd had an hour's work out on the Wii that night and not yet showered so I was particularly sweaty. Don't fret Di, Jo-Jo was asleep!

'Oh Sarah' said Mum who couldn't stop laughing. I thought

the end was nigh for her at one point!

'Oh balls to it, he deserves it'. So, Jo-Jo's wriggly worms were now more than adequately covered in my aerobic armpit sweat!

Chris came at 9.30am the next morning and Jo-Jo ran to the car with 'the bag' of wriggly sweaty worms.

'Daddy, I've saved two for you. Go on, eat them'.

'Oh thank you Johnathan'. I stood at the door, with Mum surreptitiously at my bedroom window leaning out to see Chris eat the sweat covered worms! I so wanted this moment to be in slow motion. He picked both of them out of the bag at the same time and put them in his mouth 'Mmmm they're lovely Jo-Jo, thank you'. I shot a glance up to the bedroom window to see Mum nearly in tears with laughter. I took great satisfaction in waving Jo-Jo off knowing that revenge doesn't always have to be visible or noticed by the other person. There is a saying that revenge is a dish best served cold. I am now changing that to 'revenge is a sweet best wiped on the armpit first before serving'.

Sunday, February, 2011. (Fucking Florida)

Jo-Jo and I are having dinner, he's just come back from Chris's. I'm doing my best not to interrogate him but I'm dying to know what he's done and if Hagrid had been in bed again. Apparently, she goes to bed in the afternoon whilst Chris, Jo-Jo and Joshua go out. Oh how I laughed when I heard this.

Anyway, Jo-Jo was in no mood to succumb to my interrogation so I gave up. 'Daddy took Joshua to Disneyland Paris '. I nearly choked on a sprout.

'Pardon darling? He's actually taken him to Disney? Really?' I'm trying my utmost to be nonchalant here. 'Wow, when did he do that?' Jo-Jo shrugs his shoulders.

'Can't remember. He said I couldn't go as you said I'm not allowed'. I need to pause Jo-Jo for a while whilst I swear and kick something before coming back down to earth.

'Well darling, I can honestly say to you that he's not

mentioned it to me and if he had asked me I would have said 'yes'. I changed the subject because I'm fuming. I'm not going to mention it to Chris just yet but will text him before he picks Jo-Jo up next time.

When Chris next arrived he said, 'I need to talk to you and Jo-Jo about this. Jo-Jo, what's this I hear about you telling Mummy I took Joshua to Disneyland Paris without you?' Jo-Jo started getting upset at this point. 'What we said Jo-Jo was that we are going to Florida in two years and would like to take you if Mummy says yes. You must not tell lies.'

By this time Jo-Jo is in floods and I try and console him. I also want to cry because taking him to Florida is my dream.

'Wow Jo-Jo that'll be lovely how exciting'. I'm then left on the doorstep feeling very flat. It's my dream Chris, not yours. Jo-Jo came back full of Florida and what you can do there and see. Chris had shown him a website and DVD of Florida holidays.

'You're on an aeroplane for eight hours Mummy and there's a DVD player in the seat in front of you. The theme parks are huge and they have a Harry Potter one too. I can't wait to go'. What a twat Chris is, he's not going for another two years. What's the point in doing that? All Jo-Jo can talk about now is Fucking Florida.

What annoys me more is that Chris and I went twice when we were together. We loved it so much and dreamed of taking our children and made a promise to ourselves that we would do this. It's such a magical place. I'm crying, because I'm in no position whatsoever to take Jo-Jo to Florida and neither will I be for the foreseeable future. He has such a sense of adventure and fun and I want to see his face when he enters the Magic Kingdom for the first time. Stop it Sarah, it's two years away, Hagrid could have another baby by then. I'm now saving so hard to take him before Chris, by saving my change and putting it in a pot. I don't think I'll ever save enough but it makes me feel better. I know it's probably childish and silly, but I couldn't bear him not going with me for the first time. I think I deserve it. Why should Chris just dip in and out of Jo-Jo's life when he pleases and then have the fun of taking him on a luxurious holiday? Fucking Florida.

Wednesday

Mum had had Jo-Jo overnight for me to give me a break at the weekend. I love my time with Jo-Jo but I've been craving some adult time and a break from children's TV bilge. I haven't been into town and 'mooched' around for such a long time and I was really looking forward to it. I didn't have a lot of money to spend but needed some bits and was looking forward to my fix in the 99p shop! Whoever invented these shops should be knighted, they are a God send in my opinion. Anyway, I was really enjoying a browse and looking at things in my own time. I was at the till ready to pay and a gentleman behind me said to his son, who was about seventeen, 'I hate it in here, I almost feel dirty just being here'. My natural reaction was to turn around to look at who had said such a dreadful thing. He saw me look at him. 'Don't you find this shop makes you feel dirty though love?'

'In what way?' I asked him.

'I dunno, but it's one of those shops you just hope and pray you don't walk out of and bump into someone you know'.

It was then my turn to pay for what I'd bought and I wanted the ground to open up and swallow me. I felt humiliated by this man and was hoping he wouldn't look at what I was buying. I then thought, you know what Sarah, don't be ashamed of who you are. Don't let some snobby arsehole get to you. 'Well, some people aren't obviously as fortunate as you. Some of us don't have a choice where we shop and come here out of necessity. Don't judge people because of where they shop or what they buy. This could be you one day and life has a funny way of making you learn lessons'.

I walked out of the 99p shop feeling pleased that I'd said something to the pompous git. The old Sarah would have run back to the car hoping and praying that no-one saw her with her 99p bags in her hand. Now, the liberated, 'don't take no shit' Sarah, walked out with her head held high and ample chest sticking out with full pride!

Saturday

I have come to the conclusion that I am going to be the mother-in-law from hell. I have developed a 'catch phrase', *I've done it all on my own*, obviously referring to bringing up a child. I can just picture myself with my daughter- in-law and Jo-Jo with their new born, struggling with all the new hurdles they have to face; sleepless nights, projectile vomit, high pitched screaming etc and endlessly quoting 'You don't have to tell me how hard it is, I did it on my own'. I will be saying this whilst folding my arms and having a defiant look on my face. 'If your bloody mother tells me once more how she brought you up on her own, I won't be responsible for my actions'. So, to my potential daughter-in-law, I would like to apologise in advance for being the mother-in-law from hell. I'm sure you'll be a brilliant mother, with my help!

Chapter 11

Happily Ever After

The best way to prepare for life is to begin to live.
Elbert Hubbard

Sunday, June, 2011.
Hello Di. Think I'm going to get asthma from blowing all the dust off you! I've been so busy – counselling and going to the gym! Yes dear Di, I've managed to find time, and money, to join the gym and have some *me* time. My God do I need it. I had two choices either a: keep convincing myself that my clothes have shrunk in the wash and that I'm continually retaining fluid and have a period due or b: stop eating crap and lose weight. So, I chose option b. I love it. I have panda eyes, a face that resembles an over ripe, wet, tomato and sweat from orifices I never knew existed, but I feel alive. I gave up trying to exercise at home. Jo-Jo always wants to join in but my lounge is too small for two us of and I walloped him once whilst getting over excited doing a grapevine. It was also just not worth the hassle of him moaning all the way through Dame Rosemary 'this is boring, I want to watch my telly, when will you be finished?'

My counselling is going really well. I work at three Children's Centres now, helping parents prepare mentally for birth. I was extremely nervous at first. It's proving to be beneficial though. The expectant parents complete diaries of their birth expectations versus the reality; it's amazing what people admit to worrying about. I love meeting them again when they've given birth and looking back in their diaries to compare the expectations of labour, birth and coping versus the reality of it all. From this, some women realise why they're perhaps not feeling as good as they want to be / should be and we have taken steps to turn this around.

I love what I do. My new website is up and running too, which is just so exciting. I have to say that life is pretty good and steady and I don't feel I have anything else I need to offload, rant about, document or share with you now, but I must tell you about a conversation I had with Jo-Jo today. He's nine and still finds a way to make me hyperventilate. Listen to this…

It started off all innocent and lovely and my nerves were calm. I was taking him and his friend swimming and whilst at the traffic lights, 'Take That' came on the radio. The conversation with Jo-Jo went like this…

'I love this song.'

'Who is it Mummy?'

'Take That.'

'Is it their new one?'

'Gosh no darling, this was around in, and I'm guessing here, about 1993, long before you were born. Robbie was still with them then.'

'Did Robbie leave then?'

'Yes and Take That went their own way for a while too but came back together a couple of years ago.'

'Why did Robbie leave?'

'I'm not sure now, I think they fell out for a while.'

'Did Robbie know they split up?'

'Yes, I think so.'

'What did he think of it?'

How the fuck would I know? 'I don't know darling.'

'Did they delete each other from their phones?'

'Yes,' Really regretting my innocent comment now.

'How did they get back in touch then?'

'I don't know Jo-Jo, I just said I like the song!' (But I'm now losing the will to live and if I'm not careful I may have to show you the bottom of the pool.)

Before the Take That song, all was well. I was calm, chilled out almost, and then my innocent comment turned me into a 'Tasmanian Devil'. That's the thing about being a parent; you just can't gauge whether the next thing you say is going to get either a: a one word answer; b: no answer at all; or c: the sodding Spanish inquisition.

I was talking to Sue the other day and we talked about things we never thought we'd do as a parent. Look at some of mine!

1. I can remember smugly sprouting, many times, something anal along the lines of 'my child shall only be allowed to watch the television for an hour a day, and never at meal times, that's appalling'. Every morning without fail, I'm asked, 'Can I put the television on?' My television is an unpaid entertainer/baby sitter. I love it so much, I buy it a Christmas present. That screen in the corner of the room enables me to put the washing out, have a shower, clean, read a magazine, make dinner etc. However, no matter what's on the TV, you can never, I repeat, never, make a phone call. Why oh why do children ignore you and want nothing, but as soon as you make a phone call, they decide they either need to:

a) speak to you urgently
b) decide they're starving hungry and really need a biscuit
c) want a poo
d) need a drink

2. Swear in front of my son. I'm sorry, but when you've had a bad day, or your child has turned into the anti Christ, the words 'balderdash', 'darn it', or 'gosh' don't work. There's nothing like a good 'fuck' 'shit' 'tits' and 'arse' to relieve so much tension. Jo-Jo is under the illusion that when he's eighteen he'll go to Buckingham Palace to receive a certificate to say he can swear. I think that's fair!

3. Bribe my child. 'No child will ever get the better of me. It's my way or the high way, so he or she better watch out. I'm not bargaining with my child for an easy life'. Utter bollocks. 'Jo-Jo, if you go and get your jarmies on and brush your teeth, I'll let you stay up for a bit longer'. 'Jo-Jo, do your homework now and we'll go out for an ice cream'. 'Tidy your room and you can go on the Wii for a while'. Don't let anyone try and convince you they don't bribe their children at some point during the day. It's par for the course!

So dear Diary, thanks for being there for me over the last few years, you've been such an incredible support to me. Who knows, I may need you again in a few years when Jo-Jo becomes a teenager. That's quite a scary thought. The hormones are kicking in now, so I'd best move to somewhere with a wine cellar to accommodate my medicinal alcohol requirements! Can you imagine the testosterone flying around then? He's going to be taller than me by the time he's twelve I reckon so I doubt I'll be able to boss him around.

Oh what fun and adventures do I have in store for me? Will I be on my own do you think? Will Chris still be with Hagrid, or decide to try someone else from Hogwarts and move in with Professor McGonagall?

I've come such a long way since Chris left and dealt with so much. The list is quite lengthy when you actually write it down; learning how to stand up to Chris, having the worry of not knowing if I can afford food, dealing with the NSPCC, how to play football and understand the offside rule, well sort of and I've earned myself a Diploma in Counselling. I think the main thing I've learned is to enjoy life for what it is. I don't take as much crap as I used to, that's for sure. I could have let my depression get the better of me and taken my resentment of Chris out on Jo-Jo but the events of the last nine years have brought out the true me, the me I've always wanted, and known, I could be, but never encouraged to be by Chris. I'm stronger, in control of my life and proud of the Mum and person I am. I once likened myself to a grape left on a vine never to ripen but I've come such a long way and have now ripened in to a full bodied Chardonnay!

Whatever happens, well done Sarah, I'm so very proud of you.

Me, Myself and Motherhood

Dear God above what I have done
To deserve such a wonderful son

It's not been easy as you know
In the early years I felt so low

I held on tight for a bumpy ride
On the motherhood roller coaster with you by my side

Life can be lonely, life can be sad
Some days I really thought I was going mad

I picked myself up, determined to stand tall
And learned that sometimes it's okay to fall

Motherhood is many things
With each day, a new challenge it brings

I realise now I won't always get it right
A fact I accept in my motherhood plight

I've learned to play, heal and cook
And written my experiences down in this book

Ruth E Briddon –
Mum, footballer, cook, doctor, children's entertainer, mind reader, teacher and sleep deprivation expert (this list isn't exhaustive, just very exhausting)

About the Author

Ruth Briddon gained a Diploma in Counselling with Oxford College ODL in October 2008 and is a member of the Complementary Medical Association of Great Britain. She also has a Diploma in Advanced Counselling Skills through The British School of Yoga. When her son, Alex, was born in 2003, she realised that the birth hadn't gone according to plan as her thoughts and feelings weren't that of her friends and as portrayed in the media.

When Alex was two weeks old she knew that, one day, she would qualify as a counsellor and help women through the transitional phase into motherhood. This support was unavailable when Alex was born and Ruth openly admits to not coping in the early stages of being a Mum. She needed to off load the thoughts that were consuming her, but was afraid of the consequences this would have on her and Alex.

As well as seeing private clients, Ruth currently works with local Children's Centres, giving talks to parents-to-be about preparing themselves mentally for parenthood. She talks about the expectations versus the reality of pregnancy, labour, birth and coping. The feedback she has received from the Mums-to-be has been positive and her talks have helped them to prepare mentally for the new career ahead of them.

Giving birth and being a parent is an undervalued and understated achievement and Ruth is passionate about making people realise this. You can read more about Ruth and make an appointment to see her via her website *www.postnatalsupport.com.*

Acknowledgements

They say you can't choose your family, but I'd choose mine any day. I am truly blessed with a wonderful Mum, without whom I would have been lost in recent years. Thanks Mum for your understanding, unconditional love and support. You've made me the Mum I am today. You're the best and I love you very much. x

Not only do I have the best Mum but I also have the best Sister. Thank you Paula for your advice, thoughtfulness, inspiration and kindness. Without you, this book would still be a dream. I love you very much. x. PS I'll go 52! x

My gorgeous son Alex. I know I've not always got things right and sometimes say, and do, the wrong things. This parenting lark sure is hard at times. I love you so much sweetheart and really don't know what I would do without you. x

Wendy and Terry, my lovely neighbours. Thank you for your support and kindness when I lived next door to you. It was great knowing you were there and I will always appreciate your support. x

To my friends, too many to mention, but you know who you are (including Classic FM TV). Thanks for making me laugh during the dark days and putting up with my endless crying, moaning and anxiety attacks. To my 'school Mum friends', thanks for your help and support and much valued friendship. Please note everyone that Sam 'leaves the house at half seven.' x

To my boss, Phil, and friends at work. You were so patient with me all through the bad times and I will always remember that. x

Ivybridge, Newton Abbot and Kingsbridge Children's Centres. You do such a fabulous job and I'm proud to be associated with you and honoured to work with you. Long may your good work continue. x

Kate – Thank you seems such an insignificant thing to say, but

I really couldn't have achieved this without you. You've turned me into a writer! Thank you for helping me, believing in me and sharing my dream. x

**SASSY
BOOKS**

Hip, real and raw, SASSY books share authentic truths, spiritual insights and entrepreneurial witchcraft with women who want to kick ass in life and y'know...start revolutions.